THE EXCEPTION

THE EXCEPTION

Uncle Buck's Book of Irrepressible Navigation

BARRY GIFFORD

SEVEN STORIES PRESS
NEW YORK • OAKLAND • LONDON

SEVEN STORIES PRESS
140 Watts Street
New York, NY 10013
www.sevenstories.com

College professors and high school and middle school teachers may order free examination copies of Seven Stories Press titles. Visit https://www.sevenstories.com/pg/resources-academics or email academics@sevenstories.com.

Library of Congress Cataloging-in-Publication Data is on file.

ISBN: 978-1-64421-550-0 (paperback)
ISBN: 978-1-64421-551-7 (ebook)

Printed in the USA.

9 8 7 6 5 4 3 2 1

ACKNOWLEDGMENTS

Some of these stories were originally published by Seven Stories Press (New York) in the books *Memories from a Sinking Ship* (2007), *Sad Stories of the Death of Kings* (2010), *The Roy Stories* (2013), *The Cuban Club* (2017), *Roy's World* (2020), *The Boy Who Ran Away to Sea* (2022), and *Ghost Years* (2024).

Several of the stories were published in the following magazines: *Confabulario* [*El Universal*] (Mexico City), *Narrative* (San Francisco), *Vice* (New York/London/Stockholm), *Santa Monica Review*, and *Southwest Review* (Dallas).

Drawings by Barry Gifford.

This book is for Commander Colby,
our Hector, tamer of horses

And is dedicated to the memories of
Michael Swindle and Vinnie Deserio

"Men are vain and death is long."

—Soothsayer in Akira Kurosawa's
film *Throne of Blood*

For Meridian Altitude

1. Correct H^s to obtain H^o.

2. Subtract H^o from 90° to get ZD. If in N Latitude & Sun is Bearing S, Name ZD - North.

3. Apply Declination. If Dec and ZD is same name. - ADD. If opposite name (like N & S) Subtract and take name of Larger.

Example

89° - 60'	(90°)
76° - 20'	H^o
13° - 40'	ZD - N
10° - 14°	Dec N
23° 54'	Latitude N.

Uncle Buck's notes in his copy of The Offshore Navigator by Warwick M. Tompkins (1946)

CONTENTS

AUTHOR'S NOTE

Roy's father, Rudy, died at the age of forty-eight, two months after his son's twelfth birthday. Roy's parents had divorced when he was five years old but they remained close friends. Rudy became ill two years before he died, during which time Roy saw him less frequently. Following Rudy's death, Roy's mother's brother, Buck, became Roy's patriarchal figure. Buck took his relationship with his nephew seriously and they spent a great deal of time together until Buck passed away at the age of ninety-three. *The Exception* is an elliptical chronicle of Roy's memories of his Uncle Buck.

THE EXCEPTION

UNCLE BUCK

The Exception

Tampa, Florida, was a quiet, sleepy fishing and cigar manufacturing city in the 1950s, when Roy's Uncle Buck, his mother's brother, moved there and went into the construction business. Roy enjoyed visiting Tampa, which was easy to do from either Key West or Havana, the two places Roy's mother preferred spending time when Roy was a boy, before they went to live in Chicago. Roy's mother would often leave him with her brother while she traveled elsewhere. Roy was happiest when he got to hang out with his Uncle Buck, taking fishing trips in the Gulf of Mexico or just accompanying him while he did business in Tampa.

One of Buck's closest associates was his poker buddy, Chino Valdes, who owned the Oriente Bank in Ybor City. Chino's real first name was Nestor, but everyone, including Roy, called him Chino because his narrow, slanted eyes gave him an Asian appearance.

"Know why I'm called Chino?" he asked Roy.

"No, why?"

" 'Cause my grandmother had a little yen."

Chino was a partner in a nightclub on the outskirts of Tampa named El Paraíso Bajo las Estrellas, where he and Roy's uncle often met. Buck took Roy along with him to El Paraíso several times in the afternoons, letting his nephew sit at the bar and order Coca-Colas and watch the showgirls rehearse while he and Chino discussed matters of mutual importance.

It was on one of these afternoons at El Paraíso that Roy was present during a murder, an event about which he was sworn to secrecy by his uncle and Chino Valdes.

This incident occurred the day before Roy's twelfth birthday. He and his uncle arrived at El Paraíso shortly after two in the afternoon. Chino was already there, sitting at a table by himself, sipping Matusalem rum on the rocks. Roy and Buck walked over to Chino, who stood up and shook hands with both of them, then sat down, as did Buck.

"Go watch the girls, Roy," said Chino, and handed the boy a five-dollar bill. "It's educational. The drinks are on me."

Roy smiled at Chino, thanked him, and went over to the bar and climbed up on a stool. He placed the fin down in front of him and when Alfredito, the bartender, came over, said hello and ordered a Coke. Roy liked Alfredito, a short, thin, bald-headed man with a mustache that looked like two caterpillars crawling towards one another. Alfredito never charged Roy for his drinks. The five-dollar bill that Chino gave Roy, as he did every time Roy came in, was to be left on the bar as a tip for Alfredito.

The dancers were on the stage, practicing their routines. Most of them were coffee-colored Cuban girls. They wore short shorts and little tops that left their midriffs bare. Roy thought they were all beautiful.

"How come you never look at the dancers?" Roy asked Alfredito. "You always keep your back to them."

"I'm an old man, chico," said Alfredito. "I have grandchildren older than some of these girls. It is for their sake that I don't turn around. When they look at me, I see pity in their eyes. I want to spare them the pain."

Roy remembered a story his uncle had told him after the first time they'd gone together to El Paraíso. It was about one of the dancers, a brunette originally from Matanzas named Soslaya Zancera, who was billed as the Ava Gardner of Cuba. Soslaya was the star of the show and the girlfriend of one of the owners, Morris Perlstein. One night Perlstein caught her in an unnatural embrace with the club bouncer, Roberto Bulto, in her dressing room, and shot Bulto dead. Perlstein then fired two bullets into the girl's buttocks when she attempted to flee. The owner was subsequently convicted of manslaughter and sentenced to twenty years in prison. His mistress survived, but her injuries put an end to her career as a dancer. Roy's uncle told him that Soslaya now walked with the aid of two canes and worked as a manicurist at the Hotel Khartoum in Miami Beach.

"It was a tragedy," said Buck. "Soslaya Zancera was exceptional."

Roy looked over at the table where his uncle and Chino Valdes were sitting. A third man had joined them, a large, pale-faced person wearing a mauve guayabera, a Panama hat, and dark glasses. Roy noticed that the man's fingernails were painted blood red. He had never before seen a man wearing nail polish.

"Who's that guy?" Roy asked Alfredito.

"Cherry Dos Rios," said Alfredito, "from Fort Lauderdale."

"What does he do?"

"He's in the construction business."

"Like my uncle."

Alfredito nodded, and said, "It's a good business to be in."

Roy returned his attention to the girls. Music came from a tape recorder because the band was there only at night. Alfredito told Roy the musicians slept during the day.

Suddenly, there was a loud popping sound, and the dancers stopped. Roy looked around and saw Chino Valdes hand a revolver to a man in a green seersucker suit, who walked quickly out of the club. Cherry Dos Rios sat slumped in his chair, a large, dark stain spreading under his mauve guayabera. His Panama was on the table. He still had on the dark glasses. Someone turned off the music.

Roy's uncle came over to him and said, "Vamonos, sobrino."

Chino stood up and came over, too.

"Chico," he said to Roy, placing a hand on the boy's left shoulder, "your uncle and I know that we can depend on your not having witnessed this unfortunate little accident."

Roy looked at Chino and nodded.

"Buck tells me that tomorrow is your birthday. Here's something from me."

Chino handed Roy a hundred-dollar bill. Roy had never held one before.

"If you're anything like your uncle," Chino said, "I know you'll use it well."

"Thank you," said Roy. "I will."

The dancers had disappeared. Two men were dragging Cherry Dos Rios's limp corpse into a back room. As Roy and his uncle walked together out of El Paraíso, Roy saw Alfredito pick up Cherry Dos Rios's hat off the table at which he'd been sitting. Alfredito waved it at Roy and smiled.

As Buck pulled his white 1958 Eldorado convertible onto Gasparilla Road, he asked, "Would you like me to put the top down?"

"Sure," said Roy.

His uncle unhooked the latch on his side and Roy undid the one on his, then Buck flipped a switch on the dashboard and the top peeled back. The warm Gulf air felt good on Roy's face and in his hair.

"It's time you started to think about what profession you want to go into when you get older," said his uncle. "Do you have any ideas?"

"Not yet," said Roy.

"You can't go wrong in the construction business."

"Alfredito told me the guy who accidentally got shot was in the construction business."

Roy's uncle picked a cigar out of a box he kept on the front seat next to him, bit off one end, spit the leaves out his window, and pushed in the dash lighter.

"Forget about him, Roy," said Buck. "He was the exception."

Alligator Story

A kid wearing a Tampa Tarpons t-shirt came running up the street shouting, "Some cracker just shot a gator!"

Roy and his Uncle Buck were in the driveway of the house on Oakview Terrace, rinsing down the boat. They had just come in from fishing out of Oldsmar and had been gone since five o'clock that morning; it was now six thirty in the evening. They hadn't had much luck, having boated several kingfish and a few mackerel, but they'd run on sharks everywhere and had to cut lines to get rid of them. The weather had been spotty, the water in the Gulf was cloudy, and there were periodic brief showers. It was just the two of them, so they'd had a lot of time to talk. Roy was twelve and a half years old and he loved to listen to Buck, who was forty-five. Buck was full of information on almost any subject. He was well-traveled and well-read and today he had been teaching Roy about navigation, explaining a rhumb line, which is a course that makes the same angle with each meridian which it crosses; it is constant in direction throughout and always appears as a straight line on charts.

"But the curve of shortest distance between any two points on the earth is always an arc of a great circle," Roy's uncle told him, "the sort of circle which would be marked out if we were to slice the earth into two halves, passing the cut through the ends of the course and the center of the earth. The shortest path will always be a great circle course."

Buck had been a lieutenant commander in the navy during the war and he was a civil and mechanical engineer; sometimes his explanations were too esoteric or complicated for Roy to absorb, but his uncle was always careful to show Roy what he was talking about.

"It's the wind you have to pay the closest attention to," said Uncle Buck. "The winds will control the course more than mathematical considerations."

As the kid in the Tarpons t-shirt ran by, Buck asked him, "Where's he got it?"

"On the little pier at the end of Palmetto," the kid shouted.

Buck cut off the hose and went into the utility shed and came back out with a sheathed knife and a hatchet. He handed the hatchet to Roy and said, "Come on, nephew, let's go down there."

Roy and his uncle walked along River Grove under massive hanging moss and cut across the narrow skiff launch to Palmetto Street, which they followed down to the little pier. When they got there they saw a skinny man about forty years old wearing only a pair of gray trousers with the butt of a pistol sticking out of the waistband and a dark-brown Remington Ammo cap slicing up the belly side of a six-and-a-half-foot-long alligator. The man's pants, chest, and arms were spattered with blood.

Buck and Roy watched him work for a minute, then Buck said, "What are you going to do with the hide?"

The man was working fast and he did not look up.

"Throw it away. There's a five-hundred-dollar fine you get caught with it. All I need's the meat."

Roy and his uncle and two boys who were about eight or nine years old and had been swimming in the Hillsborough River watched the man hack and tear feverishly at the carcass. It was still very hot, although the sun had begun to go down. Roy knew that it was against the law to shoot a gator without a permit; he guessed that the man didn't have permission to kill alligators, so he wanted to take what was edible and get going.

When the man had finished carving up the belly, he crammed the meat into a canvas sack, stood up and wiped his knife on his right trouser leg, and said to Buck, "I'll leave the rest to you, then."

The man walked off with the sack over his left shoulder. Roy noticed that he was barefoot and his right leg was considerably shorter than his left. The bag full of gator meat seemed to help keep him balanced as he made his way up the pebbly incline from the dock and disappeared behind the hanging moss.

Buck unsheathed his knife, flipped what remained of the alligator onto its stomach, and told Roy to chop off the head.

Roy hesitated and his uncle said, "Come on, nephew, we don't want Fish and Game to find us. Run your fingers along the top of the spine and find the soft spot."

The ridges along the gator's back were hard as stones and sharp-edged but not abrasive like a shark's skin. Roy's fingers found what felt like a seam two inches behind the head and with both hands wrapped tightly around the handle of the hatchet raised it just above his right shoulder and brought it down into where he judged the seam to be. The blade cut a half inch into the hide before meeting resistance from muscle and tendon. Roy dropped down from his squatting position and straddled the snout with a knee on either side of the gator's head resting on the planks. The two boys watched intently as Roy hacked away until the head began to separate from the rest of the body. It took about fifteen or twenty minutes to sever the head entirely. When Roy stood up his legs and arms were trembling and his hands hurt.

"Pull the head away," said his uncle, "and stand back."

Buck knelt on the gator's back from the opposite end and began cutting at the hide. Roy stood with the two boys and observed as Buck swiftly but carefully skinned the ancient-looking reptile. Sweat streamed down Roy's uncle's face as he worked, cutting evenly as he progressed from neck to tail, taking particular care not to mutilate the feet. The sun had been down for three hours before Buck completed the job. Roy and the two boys, who were cousins named Rupe and Rhett, were seated cross-legged on the pier.

"That was tough, huh?" Rupe said.

"Alligators have survived for tens of thousands of years," said Buck. "They don't live in houses, like people do, so they have to be protected from the elements."

"God made 'em tough," said Rhett.

"What you gonna do with the head?" asked Rupe.

"You can take it, if you like," Buck said.

Rupe and Rhett stood up and together they lifted the head.

"Whoa, it's heavy," said Rupe, and they dropped it. "We can't carry it all the way to my house."

"Your mama wouldn't let you keep it anyhow," said Rhett.

"Shove it into the river," said Buck.

The cousins slid the head to the end of the pier and pushed it over. There was a small splash when the head hit the water. It floated on the surface for a few seconds, then tilted backwards so that the mouth half opened and grinned at them before the head sank out of sight.

"Them were some terrible lookin' teeth," said Rhett.

Buck kicked what was left of the gator's guts, bones, and intestines into the river, then lifted the hide under the front legs.

"Grab the tail with two hands," he told Roy. "Put your arms underneath. Adiós, muchachos."

Rupe and Rhett watched Roy and his uncle carry off the hide.

Back at the house, Buck brought out from the garage a board about six feet long and three feet wide. He and Roy centered the hide on top of it, then Buck tacked it down so that it was stable. He went into the house and came back out with a box of salt and sprinkled the salt liberally all over the hide.

"Pick up the other end," Buck said, and he and Roy carried the board with the gator skin tacked to it around to the backyard and set it down on the ground. Buck took two cinder blocks and placed them down five and a half feet apart, then he and Roy picked up the board and set it down end to end on the blocks.

"It'll be all right here for now," said Buck. "The sun will hit it first thing in the morning, then we'll hoist it up onto the garage roof in the afternoon to dry out."

Buck looped his right arm around Roy's shoulders.

"You did a great job, nephew. I know that head didn't come off easily."

"You did the real work, Unk. You skinned the gator like a Seminole would."

Both Roy and his uncle were covered with blood and gristle.

"How is it you were able to keep your concentration the way you did while you were skinning him?" asked Roy. "I mean, you hardly said a word for two hours."

Buck pulled his blood-stained shirt off over his head and threw it down.

"I started thinking about your grandmother's second husband, the one who raised your mother. He hated me and I hated him and so I imagined that I was skinning him instead of the alligator."

"Why did he hate you?"

"For no good reason, really. I'm almost fourteen years older than your mother. He disliked the fact that my mother had been married before, so he resented my existence. Some men are like that; some women, too."

"Did he hate my mother?"

"No, she was a young girl, and he sent her away to school when she was old enough. I was almost a man, it was easier for him to hate me."

"My mother never talks about him; all I know is that he died."

"He had a heart attack after he and your grandmother were married for ten years; then she remarried my father."

"You must have really hated the guy to imagine that you were skinning him."

"I pretended that he was still alive but barely conscious and that he knew what I was doing but was too weak to do anything about it. I imagined that he didn't die until after I skinned him entirely."

"Did he do anything terrible to you?"

"He banished me from his house, even though my mother and sister lived there. To see me, your grandmother had to meet me somewhere else, in a park or at a restaurant. Whenever she gave me money she made me promise that he would never know that she had."

"That's crazy, Unk. How could she allow that to happen?"

"I don't know, Roy. People do all sorts of crazy things."

Buck unfastened his belt and let his pants drop to the ground. His skinning knife was in its sheath, which was still strung on the belt.

"I'm glad I never had to meet him," said Roy.

"He wouldn't have hated you, nephew. What's terrible is that I still harbor such awful feelings for a man who's been dead for twenty-five years. It's no good to keep that kind of poison in you because after awhile the poison starts to work on you. I hope you never have to hate anyone like that."

"I hope I won't, either."

"All right, let's wash up and get some dinner."

"Why didn't we save the head?"

"The only way to preserve it would be to soak it in formaldehyde. Too much trouble. The catfish are feasting on it."

"I bet those cousins are telling their folks about the alligator now."

"Come on, Roy, get your clothes off."

The head was scary, Roy thought, but it was beautiful, too. It was too bad that Rupe or Rhett hadn't kept it.

La Equivocación

After Fidel Castro's revolutionary army overthrew Cuban dictator Fulgencio Batista in 1959, Roy's Uncle Buck, who since the 1940s had been a frequent visitor to the Caribbean island, decided to go there to see what was happening with the new regime in power. Accompanied by his father, Roy's grandfather Pops Colby, who was eighty years old, Buck flew them down from his home in Tampa, Florida, to Havana, where they checked into the Riviera Hotel, which was owned and operated by the mobster Meyer Lansky.

The second day they were in the Cuban capital, walking along the Malecón, two camouflage-uniformed rebel soldiers grabbed Buck by his arms and told him he was under arrest. In fluent Spanish Buck asked them what the problem was. The soldiers did not reply but forced Buck and Pops to go with them to army headquarters. As it turned out, Buck had been mistaken for one of Batista's generals, to whom he bore a startling resemblance. The commandant at the military office ridiculed the two soldiers and ordered them to release their captives. He laughed at the possibility that a hunted enemy general would be openly strolling on the waterfront sidewalk in the company of an elderly man.

After convincing the commandant that he and his father were American tourists, Buck forgave the soldiers for their mistake and picked up a pack of cards from the commandant's desk. He briskly shuffled the cards and proceeded to perform a few magic tricks he had learned as a boy when for a time he'd been an assistant to The Great Blackstone. For years Buck had stored a large black steamer trunk full of magic props Harry Blackstone had given to him in the garage behind Roy and his mother's house in Chicago. On his occasional visits to Chicago, Buck opened the trunk and showed Roy and his friends some tricks but he never explained them, telling the kids that secrets could never be revealed except to other serious practitioners of the art.

The Cubans were charmed and amused by Buck's sleight of hand, and the commandant showed him and Pops a photograph of the general for whom he had been mistaken—and nearly shot, as one of the soldiers admitted. Buck's swarthy complexion, wavy black hair, and pencil-line mustache, the commandant told him, made him an almost dead ringer. The men laughed together and the commandant apologized and suggested that the three of them go for a drink at the government's expense, to which Buck readily agreed. At the bar of the Hotel Inglaterra, close by the Capitolio building, in which the army headquarters was housed, the commandant ordered for all of them.

"What did he order?" Pops, who did not understand Spanish, asked Buck.

"Cuba libres, of course," said Buck. "What else?"

When Buck and Pops got back to Chicago and told Roy and his mother what happened, Roy, who was twelve years old, asked his uncle if he had been afraid the soldiers might shoot him.

"Not really, they were just doing their duty. It was the commandant I was worried about. If he'd been a younger guy who hated the United States, like Che Guevara, he wouldn't have thought twice about throwing me into Morro prison or putting me in front of a firing squad in Gran Stadium along with other extranjeros suspected of being spies. I heard that Guevara himself shot thirty-five men in one day."

"What about you, Pops?" Roy asked. "Were you afraid?"

"I'm an old man, Roy. I'm too old to be afraid."
"How old do you have to be to not be afraid of anything?"
Buck laughed and said, "Sobrino, it's never too soon to start."

Tris Speaker's Memory

Pops, Roy's grandfather, his mother and Uncle Buck's father, was an avid baseball fan. He'd seen most of the great major league players in action during the 1920s, '30s, '40s, and now the '50s. He told Roy about Babe Ruth, Lou Gehrig, Ty Cobb, and others and singled out Tris Speaker, a center fielder for Cleveland in the early and mid-twenties, as his favorite among them.

"Speaker patrolled the outfield like an eagle, swooping down and chasing after flyballs as if they were predators prowling around the nest looking to snatch the eaglets. Graceful, Tris was, he played shallow, fast, took perfect angles toward the ball. He threw and batted lefthanded, hit .380 when he was thirty-five, good enough arm. Keen eye—like Cobb and later Joe DiMaggio disdained pitches even a fraction off the plate. I wish you could have seen him, Roy, nobody like him now. Had some trouble once, though, he and Cobb were accused of throwing a game but it didn't stick."

Pops was in his late seventies and early eighties when he described for Roy the exploits of baseball players he'd observed, some almost half a century before. Roy wanted to know how his grandfather could still remember them so vividly.

"Well, babe, there are many theories about how and why some people remember things better or worse than others. I believe that a person rarely forgets something or someone he or she especially likes or dislikes. That and repetition. When you keep doing something in particular it becomes a part of you. For example, Tris Speaker ran down thousands of flyballs in hundreds of ballparks. He enjoyed doing this, and of course this attention to detail benefited him in his profession, he excelled in order to make a living, to be well paid. Repetition informed by terrific foot speed and superior eyesight. Depth perception in his case was especially important. He made the most of these God-given gifts."

"How does God decide who to give the gifts to?" Roy asked.

Pops smiled and shook his head.

"That's a mystery, Roy, one for the scientists to figure out. Maybe you'll be a great scientist and discover why."

"I'd rather be a great baseball player," said Roy.

Wanted Man

The summer I was thirteen years old I worked in Cocoa Beach, Florida, building roads and houses for my uncle's construction company. One afternoon when we were paving a street in 105-degree heat, a police car pulled up to the site, stopped, and two cops got out, guns drawn. They moved swiftly toward the steamroller, which was being operated by Boo Ruffert, a former Georgia sheriff. The cops proceeded without a word and grabbed Boo, dragging him down from his perch atop the steamroller. I was shoveling limerock off of a curb directly across from the action, and I watched the cops handcuff Ruffert and begin double-timing him toward their beige and white. Jake Farkas, who had been sweeping behind Boo, jumped up onto the steamroller and shut it down before the machine went out of control and careened off the road. My uncle came running out of the trailer he used as an office and intercepted the policemen before they locked Boo Ruffert into the patrol car.

"Wait!" my uncle shouted at the cops. "What are you doing with him?"

"This man is wanted on a charge of child molestation in Georgia," said one of them. "We have a warrant for his arrest."

"Want to see it?" asked the other cop. He was holding the nose of his revolver against Ruffert's right temple.

"Listen," said my uncle, "Boo here is my best heavy equipment operator. He's almost finished with this street."

My uncle pulled out a roll of bills from one of his trouser pockets.

"Let me buy you fellows some lunch. Ruffert won't go anywhere, I'll keep an eye on him. You boys have something to eat while he finishes up here."

He held two fifties out toward them. "How about it?"

The cops looked at the money in my uncle's hand, then stuffed Ruffert into the back seat.

"Sorry," said one, "you'll have to get yourself another man. This one's headed to the hoosegow."

I had walked over and stood watching and listening to this exchange. I looked at Ruffert through the left side rear window. Boo grinned at me, exposing several brown teeth, and winked his right eye, the one with the heart-shaped blood spot on the lower outside corner of the white. I guessed Boo's age to be about forty. Jake Farkas came up and stood next to me. Jake always had the stub of a dead Indian, as he called cigars, in his mouth, usually a Crook, and three or four days' worth of whiskers on his face. He was in his early thirties but had already fathered, he told me, approximately thirteen children.

"You think you can ride her down the rest of the way?" my uncle asked Jake.

"Sure thing," Jake said.

My uncle turned and walked back to the trailer.

"Did you know about Boo?" I asked. "That he was a wanted man?"

Jake chuckled and said, "My dear old Mama used to say it's always good to be wanted, but I'm older now and I know that my dear old Mama weren't always right."

Jake strode to the steamroller, hopped up into the seat, and cranked it over. I went back to shoveling limerock.

That evening, after my uncle dropped me off at a local movie theater while he went off to play cards, a bizarre incident occurred. I figured he was going to see a woman and that he knew I knew but seeing as how he had a wife in Miami, I assumed he thought it prudent not to tell me any more than he had to. I was not particularly fond of my aunt; my uncle knew this and most probably also knew I would never have betrayed his confidence had he chosen to tell me the truth, but this way neither of us had to compromise ourselves.

The movie was *Zulu*, which depicted red-jacketed, heavily armed British soldiers in South Africa battling against Shaka's spear-throwing warriors. The theater was segregated; white patrons were seated downstairs and black patrons were seated in the balcony. This was in 1964, so some small progress had been made regarding racial equality in Florida in that both whites and blacks were at least allowed to be in the movie theater together.

The redcoats were vastly outnumbered by the Zulus, but their highly disciplined British square defense—one line kneeling and firing as the line behind them stood and cleaned and reloaded their rifles—kept the natives at bay. The outcome, however, was inevitable; at some point the Zulus would overwhelm them. As the battle raged, there came from the balcony increasing shouts of exhortation directed at the Zulus, which incited equally fervent vocalizing by the white members of the audience below. The din inside the theater grew louder and more and more heated, practically drowning out the soundtrack of the picture.

Suddenly, the lights in the theater came on and the film stopped. The cinema manager jumped up onstage and stood in front of the screen. He was a large, mostly bald, clean-shaven white man wearing a baggy green suit. He held a lit cigarette between the second and third fingers of his right hand, the one he used to gesticulate and point toward the balcony. The crowd was silent.

"Listen up!" he shouted. "Any further ruckus and I'm throwin' all you niggers out of here!"

The manager kept his two cigarette fingers pointed at the balcony section for at least twenty seconds longer; then he put them to his mouth, took a long drag on the cigarette, exhaled smoke so that it curlicued slowly away from him and vanished in the lights, and dropped the butt to the floor, where he ground it out with his right shoe. He did not lower his eyes from the cheap seats until he jumped down from the stage and unhurriedly proceeded up the center aisle and out into the lobby. The sound of the doors swinging shut was the only noise in the theater until the house lights blinked out and the projector resumed rolling.

The film ended with Shaka's Zulus acknowledging the bravery and ingenuity of the British regulars by saluting them and deciding against slaughtering them wholesale, thereby emerging victorious by having made the grandest and noblest heroic gesture possible before disappearing over a distant rise. I waited until almost every other patron had left the theater before I did. There was no trouble outside. The manager stood in front of the ticket booth, smoking. Up close, I could see several dark stains on the jacket and pants of his suit.

My uncle was parked in front of the theater. I climbed into his white Cadillac convertible and he drove away.

"How was the show?" he asked.

"Good," I said, "there was lots of fighting. Did you win?"

"Win?"

"Yeah, at the poker game."

"A little," said my uncle. "I always win a little."

We drove for a while without saying anything, then I asked, "What do you think will happen to Boo?"

"He'll do some hard time, I'm sure," my uncle said. "It's a bad business, messing with children."

"Was it a boy or a girl that he messed with?"

"A girl."

"How old was she?"

"Jake told me she was ten."

"How does he know?"

"What difference does it make? Ruffert was a wanted man, you won't ever see him again. Tell me more about the movie."

Advantages

"After the war, I lived in Los Angeles for a couple of years. I worked as an engineer for the City of Van Nuys. One night I was having dinner with a girl at the Brown Derby when a girlfriend of hers came over to our table with her date. They sat down and introduced themselves to me. The man with her was Howard Hughes, the aircraft manufacturer, who was then owner of RKO Pictures. He was producing films and sometimes directing them. At the time he had a big hit, *The Outlaw*, starring Jane Russell's bosom."

Buck Colby and his twelve-year-old nephew, Roy, were having lunch in Cuervo's Silver Ring, a Cuban restaurant in the Ybor City section of Tampa, Florida, in August of 1958. A hurricane was approaching the Gulf of Mexico so they were eating fast in order to get home and tape up the windows of Buck's house before the storm hit.

"What do you mean, Unk?" Roy asked.

"Jane Russell had big breasts and Hughes, who directed the movie, made sure to show them off as often and as much of them as possible. He even designed and had constructed a brassiere for her to wear in the picture to take advantage of her assets. Some theaters refused to play the movie, and organizations such as The Legion of Decency labeled it obscene and urged that it be banned from exhibition. Of course this only served to pique people's interest, especially men's, and it broke box office records."

"Did you talk to Howard Hughes about it?"

Howard Hughes's date

"Not really. He was already reputed to be one of the richest men in the world, so we discussed business and talked about airplanes. He was a pilot, too, and I had trained to be one at the Naval Air Station in Texas."

"I didn't know you were a flier, Unk."

"I washed out, Roy, I didn't qualify, but I knew a little about airplanes."

"Was that actress—"

"Jane Russell?"

"Was she with him at the restaurant?"

"No, he was with a different actress, a very beautiful girl with dark Oriental eyes. I don't remember her name, but later I saw her in a movie where she turned into a cobra when she wanted to murder someone."

"How rich was he?"

"He'd inherited a fortune from his father, along with the Hughes Tool Company in Texas. He built it up and diversified his holdings, buying RKO and investing in gambling casinos and real estate, among many other things. At dinner he ordered two or three bottles of expensive champagne, then left me with the check. The girls drank most of the champagne, and I had a glass, but Hughes didn't. He said he never touched alcohol."

"If he was so rich, why didn't he at least split the bill with you?"

Buck laughed. "Some wealthy men—and women—are like that, Roy. They're afraid of being taken advantage of."

"You always pay for our meals."

"I don't have as many actresses to support. Finish your sandwich, nephew, the storm's beginning to come in."

La Sorpresa

Roy's father had been in Havana for a week before Roy and his mother arrived. Roy liked Cuba, having gone there for the first time the year before. Now he was about to celebrate his sixth birthday at Los Siete Pecados, La Habana's most famous nightclub. His father was friends with the owners, one of whom, Martine Finura, a short, middle-aged, large-breasted, pancake-makeup-laden woman with architecturally challenging high-piled raven-black hair, greeted Roy with a hug and a lipstick-smearing kiss and told him the night was his, that he could order whatever he wanted to eat or drink, with the exception of alcohol, of course. It was eight-thirty when he and his father entered the club.

"Rudy, where is your beautiful wife esta noche?" Martine asked. "She is coming later for when we have the birthday sorpresa?"

"Kitty's not feeling well, Martine. She won't be coming but told me to give you her best wishes, como siempre. Perhaps you'll see her before she and Roy return to Cayo Hueso. They're staying with me at the Nacional."

Roy's parents were divorced but remained on good terms, and Rudy continued to support Kitty and their son financially. Kitty's fragile health required that she reside in a temperate climate and avoid unnecessary aggravation, so she chose for the time being to live in Key West, Florida, rather than in Chicago, where Roy was born and Rudy maintained his headquarters and primary home. His business interests took him on a regular basis to Las Vegas,

New York, New Orleans, Havana, and elsewhere. Roy missed seeing his father more frequently but Rudy kept in close touch by phone and when they were together they always had a good time. Roy enjoyed meeting the wide variety of people to whom his father introduced him, though he seldom understood what their professions were.

As the premier nightclub in Havana, Los Siete Pecados showcased the most glamorous and best dancers along with the finest orchestra and entertainers, such as Pérez Prado, Benny Moré, and Americanos Nat "King" Cole, Frank Sinatra, Louis Armstrong, and others. Attached to the club and restaurant was an annex that housed a casino and bar that stayed open twenty-four hours and never closed, even on religious holidays. On this particular night Roy was doubtless the only six-year-old present. Once the floor show began, his father told him he had to go talk to some people and that he would be back soon. Martine Finura escorted Roy to a table in front of the stage and sat down next to him. Roy ordered a cheeseburger and iced Coca-Cola in a chimney-sized glass.

After he'd finished eating and there was a break in the entertainment, the orchestra played "Happy Birthday" and a voluptuous showgirl wearing a dazzling, glass-diamond-decorated headdress and a skimpy costume brought to the table a large cake with seven lit candles on it. "Una para que traiga buena suerte!" she whispered loudly in Roy's right ear. Martine told him to make "un deseo grande" and then blow out the candles, which he did with one breath. The showgirl gave Roy kisses on both cheeks and the other patrons sang along with the orchestra and then applauded. Roy asked the showgirl what her name was and she said, "I am called 'La hija de la noche,' but now that you and I are friends you may call me Lavinia."

"I hope you're still here when I'm older," Roy said, and she and Martine laughed. Lavinia kissed him again, this time on the lips, and then she was gone.

The orchestra began to play "Take Me Out to the Ballgame" and Sebastiano "El Furioso" Segura, the star center fielder for the Havana Sugar Kings professional baseball team, came to Roy's table carrying a big box. The orchestra leader announced over the microphone that Segura was presenting "un gran regalo" to Roy, a Sugar Kings uniform with the number six and Roy's name on the back of the jersey. Martine helped Roy open the box and together they removed the uniform and held it up for the audience to see. Sebastiano Segura placed a black cap with the white capital letter H above the bill on Roy's head and shook his hand. People in the crowd shouted, "Arriba! Arriba!" and Roy stood up on his chair next to Segura, who wrapped his left arm around his shoulders and waved to everyone.

The band broke from the baseball song into "Siboney" and the patrons returned their attention to the stage. Sebastiano Segura again shook hands with Roy. The ballplayer, who a few years before had played for the Pittsburgh Pirates in the major leagues but was subsequently banned for gambling and conspiring to throw games, said to Roy, "Remember, hijo, the next best thing to playing and winning is playing and losing." He laughed and exchanged besitos with Martine Finura, waved once more, and left the club.

"Feliz cumpleaños, chico," Martine said. "How do you like your sorpresa?"

"Thank you, señora," Roy said, "I've never had a real baseball uniform before."

He looked around the room.

"I wish my dad had been here to meet Sebastiano Segura and see my gift. Do you know where he is?"

Martine stood up. "Stay here, Roy. I will find him." She signaled to a waiter to come over and ordered him to bring Roy another Coca-Cola.

Roy sat holding the Sugar Kings uniform and watched the

dancers. Lavinia was in the center, in front of the others, kicking the highest. After a few minutes, a singer came onstage and the audience applauded wildly. Roy suddenly felt sleepy and rested his head on the table. He awoke as his father was carrying him to his car and laying him down gently on the back seat. A man Roy had never seen before was standing next to the car holding the box the uniform had come in.

"Put it into the trunk," Rudy told him.

Rudy closed the rear door on the passenger side then walked around the front of the car, got into the driver's seat, and started the engine. He turned his head and looked at Roy.

"I bet you'll never forget this birthday," he said.

Kitty, 1957

"They just said on the radio that Barney Ross died."

Kitty turned it off.

"I remember your dad used to help Barney out, when he was on the hop."

"Who was he?"

"A boxer, one of the best. Lightweight and welterweight champ. Jewish boy from Chicago. His father had a vegetable stand on Maxwell Street until he got shot and killed during a holdup. Made Barney an orphan at twelve, a little older than you are now, so he became a fighter. Played a good piano. He and I used to mix it up together at parties, show tunes, mostly. Always smiling. He was a war hero, your dad kept Barney's medals in the safe at his store so he wouldn't hock 'em. Your dad gave him a hypo now and again but mostly cash to buy hop. He got addicted to morphine in the army hospital. You know your dad never loaned anybody money, only gave it to people he liked or felt sorry for."

"Uncle Buck told me that, too."

"Barney was a sweetheart. His father was a rabbi, I think."

"How did he die?"

"Cancer, they said. Young, only in his fifties. After 1946, '47, I didn't see him. By then I had you to take care of, I didn't go to parties."

"He lived longer than Dad."

"Those guys lived hard. The good ones, too, like Barney and

your dad. Times were different. You won't have to do the things they did."

Kitty drove her Roadmaster convertible into South Water Market, parked near the entrance, and got out. Roy did, too.

"Good thing we kept the top up, it's starting to rain."

"Ma, there's a No Parking sign, you'll get a ticket."

"Don't worry, Roy, everyone here knew your dad."

Fencing

"You know, Mom, Uncle Buck is a lot like Zorro."

"You mean the Spanish bandit?"

"Zorro isn't a bandit, he robs the evil government officials and distributes the money to poor people."

"Buck isn't a Spaniard."

"No, but he looks like one. He's handsome like Zorro, he has a thin mustache and black hair and knows how to fence. Remember when he taught Johnny McLaughlin and me how to fence in the backyard? His foils and masks are in the black steamer trunk he keeps in our garage."

"My brother is a dashing guy. He loves you and I'm glad he teaches you things your father didn't have time to do."

"Could Dad fence?"

Kitty laughed. "No, of course not. But he could do lots of other things. It's too bad he died before he had a chance to show you. Buck likes doing things with you."

"He wants me to go to Cuba with him."

"You and your dad had good times there. I miss it, too."

"I'd rather live in Havana than here in Chicago. Chico Fernandez and I used to fence with fishing rods."

Kitty thought sometimes that she should get married again. Her brother lived in Florida now, so Roy didn't see him often. A boy needs a father, her mother said. Maybe, but she didn't need a husband. Not yet, anyway. What if Roy and whomever she married didn't get along? She didn't want to think about it.

"How about him?" June DeLisa said to Kitty while they were sipping champagne at Marva Gillespie's cocktail party.

"What about who?"

"Burt Phillips. He and Diane Cortez are on the outs now."

"So?"

"He's always gone for you. And he's loaded."

"When Marva introduced him to me, he asked where I bought my clothes. I thought that was weird."

"What did you say?"

"I asked him where he bought his."

June DeLisa laughed.

"And he doesn't in the least resemble Tyrone Power. I didn't like him."

"Why Tyrone Power?"

"He plays Zorro, Roy's favorite."

"Your brother looks a little like Tyrone Power. Uh oh, here comes Burt Phillips."

"June," he said, "you're looking dangerous, as usual."

"Hello, Burt. You know Kitty, of course."

Before he could say anything, Kitty asked him, "What distinguishes a foil from an épée?"

Phillips stared at Kitty for a few seconds, then walked away.

"Kitty," said June, "you're too cruel."

Kitty took a sip of champagne, then said, "Roy wouldn't like him, either."

Hasta Cuando

"Both Nanny and my mother were good piano players and singers. Did you ever play any instruments, Unk?"

"No, Roy. I never had the time to learn or the interest, I guess. My sister took after our mother, she had lessons from the time she was little."

"Nanny used to have me sing with her while she played and taught me to read the notes. She had a nice voice."

"I remember being in Havana with your father and mother. You were there, too. We were at the Hotel Nacional, where your father always stayed. Late one night in the bar your dad made your mother get up and play something on the piano. This was about eight years ago. You were only four or five, asleep upstairs in your room. The hotel owners were friends of your father's, they didn't mind Kitty playing if she felt like it."

"I bet she was nervous."

"There weren't many people there, it was probably two or three in the morning. She played a Cuban number, 'Quizas? Quizas?'—Who knows?—and sang it, too. She said that she'd learned the song after hearing Nat 'King' Cole sing it at the Chez Paree in Chicago."

"Did the people in the bar like it?"

"I think so, especially since she sang the lyrics in Spanish. The woman in the song is asking the man how long their love will last—'Hasta cuando?' Until when?—and he answers, 'Who knows?' "

"That was before my parents got divorced."

"Yes, that's right. They separated almost a year later."

"Maybe she chose to sing that song because she was thinking about their marriage."

"It was a popular tune at the time, lots of singers had it in their repertoire. An unconscious choice, perhaps."

Roy was one of the very few kids in his neighborhood in Chicago who came from what was commonly referred to as a broken home. He often became embarrassed when people said this, but there was nothing he could do about it.

"Boxers get knocked unconscious, Unk."

"That's different, nephew. Sometimes a thought comes into a person's mind without their meaning or wanting it to. There's no way to explain it."

Once, years later, Roy was in a restaurant when a recording of "Quizas? Quizas?" began playing. He got up without saying anything to the people he was with and walked out.

"Why did Roy leave?" one of them asked, and somebody else at the table said, "Who knows?"

In the Name of the Father

"How do you know that Superman's a Jew?"

"He comes from a faraway country, don't he? All the Jews in Chicago come from Europe, some place like that."

"Superman comes from another planet, that's farther away than Europe."

Roy and his friend Tommy Cunningham were sitting on the grass in the outfield at Green Briar Park waiting for other kids to arrive to play ball. It was July of 1954, both boys were seven years old.

"You told me your dad's from a country in Europe where he lived with Gypsies."

"Yeah, so?"

"He's a Jew."

"Your parents came over from Ireland, that's in Europe, too."

"Yeah, but we're Catholic, not Jewish."

"My mother's Catholic, and my dad doesn't have super powers."

"You should ask him if he knew anyone in his old country that did. How old was he when he came to America?"

"Ten. He couldn't speak English then."

When Roy got home later that afternoon his mother, Kitty, and her brother, Buck, were sitting at the kitchen table drinking coffee.

"Ma, when Dad lived in the old country do you think he knew anybody who was like Superman?"

"What a crazy question, Roy. Of course not. Why would you ask that?"

"Tommy Cunningham thinks Superman is Jewish because he comes from Europe, like Dad."

"Isn't Superman supposed to be from a planet named Krypton?" Kitty said. "He's not a real person, anyway."

"If Superman had been in Europe," said Roy's uncle, "he would have prevented Hitler from murdering six million Jews."

The next day Tommy told Roy, "I asked my father about Superman and he said no Dubliner he knows wears a cape, but he couldn't swear that one or more might not be able to fly if he has enough drink in him."

Tommy Cunningham's father

History Lesson

"Ten years ago, in New York City, I was invited to sit in on a meeting in a room at the Sheraton Hotel on Seventh Avenue. I was out of the navy by then. This was in 1946."

"The year I was born."

"Yes, Roy. Before the war, beginning in 1937, when I was twenty-six, I was working for the Office of Strategic Services, the OSS, under the direction of a man named Stevenson. This was before it was renamed the CIA, the Central Intelligence Agency. I was sent to Northern Ireland, where I lived for a time in Derry."

"What did you do there?"

"Our government wanted me to talk to people, listen to what they were saying. It was believed that Ireland was disposed to side with Germany if there was a war in which the United States would become involved."

Buck was driving back to Tampa from Oldsmar, where he and his twelve-year-old nephew, Roy, had come ashore after having spent the day fishing from Buck's boat, *Black Marlin*. They'd caught a few yellowtail which Roy's uncle planned to grill for dinner. Roy had been asking Buck about what he'd done during the war.

"Did you find out anything important?"

"Oh, bits and pieces. You don't know what might fit somewhere. The British had their own undercover people there, too, of course. Any information I gathered that I thought could be useful I turned over to them."

"So you were a spy."

"Sort of."

"What did Ireland have to do with the meeting in New York?"

"Nothing, other than the government kept me on board to find out some other things of interest. The meeting at the Sheraton was attended by several of the organized crime heavies called in by Meyer Lansky to help supply guns and ammunition to the Irgun in Palestine. The Irgun was a terrorist group working to establish a Jewish state in a territory controlled by the British that was populated mostly by Arabs."

"Israel, right?"

"Yes, Roy, what came to be called Israel in 1948. Lansky was Jewish and he was asking the Sicilian and Italian mafiosi to contribute money for his cause."

"Did they?"

Meyer Lansky

"To some degree. The Mafia and the Camorra had no particular stake in establishing a homeland for the Jews but these were men Lansky did business with on a regular basis in places like Havana and Las Vegas."

"Were they friends?"

"Not exactly, but they needed each other, especially in gambling enterprises. Also, the mafiosi, especially Lucky Luciano, assisted the United States government during the war, identifying traitors on the New York docks, which his mob controlled."

"How did you get into the meeting at the hotel?"

"I'd helped Lansky in dealings with the government."

"He trusted you."

"He didn't trust anybody. He wanted me to explain to the government that what he was doing for the Irgun was in our interest since the United States was supporting the creation of a Jewish state in the Middle East."

"Gee, Unk, you're part of history."

"I followed orders. I did what I was asked to do."

"You didn't get killed."

Buck laughed. "No, I didn't."

"Do you still do stuff like that for the government?"

"I'm an ordinary citizen these days, Roy."

"Did you ever feel that you were really in danger?"

Buck did not answer Roy right away. They rode along in silence for a minute before his uncle said, "Sure, I did. But I knew when to keep my mouth shut. That's probably the most important thing to be able to do."

"I'll try to remember that, Unk."

Black Soup

"Well, Roy, near the equator the sun is behind clouds more than half the day. French sailors call the equatorial belt *pot au noir*, black soup, a kind of curtain or canopy that shields the earth from the sun. Above this canopy the sun might be shining, and rain may be falling on the jungle below."

"Did you learn about weather conditions when you were in the navy?"

"Some of them, but mostly from reading and sailing, of course. It's important to know what you're getting into before going there."

"Or you might decide to not go there."

"Right. The same applies to everyday life, not only when you're navigating the equator."

Roy liked talking with his Uncle Buck, his mother's brother, more than anybody else. He often stayed at Buck's house in Florida on holidays. Roy was eleven years old when his uncle, who had sailed boats all over the world, told him about the black sky over the equator. When he went back home to Chicago, where he lived with his mother, Roy told his friend Johnny Ryan about it.

"Do you believe everything your uncle tells you?" Johnny asked him.

"Sure. Why would he want to make stuff up?"

"How does he know what French sailors call it? Does he speak French?"

"I think he does, a little, anyway. He speaks Spanish really well, he taught me some."

"Can you say black soup in Spanish?"

"I can't remember," said Roy. "I'll look it up tonight."

Later, Roy asked his mother what made Buck different from other people.

"Curiosity," she said. "My brother has always wanted to know about everything and go everywhere."

The next day Roy told Johnny Ryan, "*Sopa negra*."

being placed on the left, and those of the products on the right, of the sign = or →, which should be read "give," not "equal to."
e·qua'tion [illegible] *Gram.* A sentence, as in Latin and Russian, in which subject and predicate are not linked by a verb (L. *spes mea Christus*, Christ [is] my hope); — called also *nominal sentence.*
e·qua'tor (ē·kwā'tẽr), *n.* [LL. *aequator* one who equalizes.] **1.** *Geog.* An imaginary great circle on the earth's surface, everywhere equally distant from the two poles, dividing the earth's surface into the Northern and Southern Hemispheres. **2.** *Astron.* The great circle (***celestial equator***) in which the plane of the earth's equator intersects the celestial sphere; — so called because, when the sun is crossing it, day and night are everywhere of equal length. **3.** Any circle dividing the surface of a body into two equal and symmetrical parts, in the manner of the equator of a sphere.
e'qua·to'ri·al (ē'kwȧ·tō'rĭ·ăl; 70), *adj.* **a** Of or pertaining to the equator or an equator. **b** Resembling conditions at the equator, esp. in climate; as, *equatorial* heat. — *n. Astron.* A telescope so mounted as to have [illegible] at right angles, one of them (the polar axis) parallel to the earth's axis.
eq'uer·ry (ĕk'wẽr·ĭ; ē·kwĕr'ĭ), *n.*; *pl.* -RIES (-ĭz). [F. *écurie* stable,

The Bogotá Lift

Roy, who was fifteen, and his cousin Kip, nineteen, were working on a construction job for Kip's father, Buck, in North Tampa, Florida, next to the Seaboard railroad tracks. The boys were setting trusses on the roof of one of the four townhouses their crew were building when Buck pulled onto the construction site in a brand new white 1962 Cadillac Eldorado. Buck had been away for two weeks to Bogotá, Colombia, where he'd gone to have a face lift after reading about a surgeon there who claimed to have invented a method of plastic surgery that did not require the breaking of bones. The surgeon's price for this operation was half of that charged by doctors in the United States.

Buck was wearing large-framed glasses with dark tinted lenses. His cheeks, chin, and forehead were bright red. He was wearing a new blue suit with a shiny white shirt and an orange-colored tie. He had also dyed his hair.

"How are you boys doing?" Buck asked. "Did Witherspoon finish the staircases?"

Buck inspected the winding steps leading to the upper floor of the townhouse on which Kip and Roy were working.

"He didn't get the angles right," he said.

Buck walked back to his car, opened the trunk, took off his suit jacket and tossed it in. He then lifted out a toolbox and walked back to the townhouse and began prying up the staircase steps, repositioning and tacking them down.

That night at dinner, Buck, who did not remove his sunglasses, informed the boys that Dr. Pasmoso would be arriving in Tampa the next day.

"He's the man who did my face lift. Very clever guy. We came up with a business plan for him to set up a practice in Tampa."

"Does he have a medical license to operate here?" asked Kip.

"A local physician will be present. Pasmoso will supervise. José doesn't have a license in Colombia either, he just invented the method."

"Is he a real doctor?" Roy asked.

"He's got a degree from a school in Asunción, Paraguay. We can work out the angles."

"Just like the staircases," said Kip.

The Colombia cosmetic wizard moved in with Buck and together they set up the gambit, as Kip called it. Pasmoso was a small, thin, middle-aged man with dark brown skin and three-inch-long scars on both cheeks. He spoke only a few words of English.

"How did he get those scars?" Kip asked his father. "They can't be good advertising. Shouldn't he fix his own face?"

"How he looks has nothing to do with what he does," said Buck. "He told me he got the scars from a fencing duel when he was young."

The first thing Buck and Pasmoso did was rent office space in a shopping center not far from Buck's construction company office. Buck then designed an advertisement to place in the Tampa area telephone directory and in the local newspapers:

THE BOGOTÁ LIFT
Painless Face Lift Procedure Developed and Performed
by Dr. José Pasmoso
Instantaneous Results and No Broken Bones!

Buck paid for the ads and the first and last months' rent. His agreement with Pasmoso called for a split of the take after expenses to be thirty-five percent to Buck and sixty-five percent for the South American surgeon. Pasmoso's method consisted entirely of burning the face with refrangible, ultraviolet rays, reshaping and smoothing fatty tissue and wrinkles from front to back, gathering skin behind the ears and at the back of the neck. The only cutting was of epidermal excess behind the head.

Business built slowly at first but began picking up quickly after a few weeks as satisfied patients, mostly women, spread the word. Pasmoso rented an apartment for himself. Buck—having shed his dark glasses after ten days—concentrated on his construction projects. The only real change Kip and Roy recognized about Buck's face was that the skin around his eyes was pulled back tightly, giving him an Asiatic appearance. Buck said he had to shave now behind his ears.

All seemed to be going well until Pasmoso was arrested for attempted rape of one of his patients while she was undergoing treatment. The "local physician"—who was actually a pharmacist, not a doctor—claimed to have been out of the room at the time of the purported incident. It turned out that the dubious surgeon had entered the United States illegally, using a Brazilian passport with a different name. The medical college from which he claimed to have received his degree was revealed to have been a mail-order operation that had long since gone out of business.

Roy and Kip asked Buck if he had visited his erstwhile partner in jail. The Bogotá Lift office, of course, was closed down by order of the Hillsborough County Health Department.

"Yes, briefly. I got him a lawyer. It doesn't look good."

"Is he guilty?"

"Apparently the woman has a good case. Pasmoso's semen was found on her legs."

"What'll happen to him?"

"He'll serve time here in Florida, then be deported. It's too bad, his customers were mostly pleased with the results of their treatment. It was a good bargain."

Kip laughed. "I guess the Bogotá Lift consisted of more than this lady bargained for."

"What about your next face lift, Unk?" asked Roy. "You said Pasmoso's fix would last only two years."

"I haven't thought about it yet," said Buck.

Later, Roy said to Kip, "Your dad must have known Pasmoso was a phony."

"Maybe. I asked him if he felt betrayed by Pasmoso, and he said, 'After my gall bladder operation, they stuck a drain in my abdomen. Two weeks later, when the doctor pulled it out, it felt like a snake bit me from the inside.' "

The Secret

"I had a Cuban Chinese guy working for me for a while, Mah Sam. He was a genius plumber. Born in Shanghai; emigrated to Cuba via Hong Kong when he was nineteen or twenty. Sam was everybody's friend, spoke English and Spanish as well as Mandarin, probably Cantonese, too. Learned building trades in Havana, then hightailed it to Tampa after Castro took over. He had his hand in the rackets, too—opium, prostitution, protection, gambling—when he got in with Trafficante. It was Santo who took him to Tampa."

"Is he still around?"

"Unfortunately, no. I never found out the details, but apparently Sam got caught with the underage daughter of a Chinese grocer who shot him. Hated to lose Mah Sam, he could make water run uphill where nobody else could. He was a character, told me he only went for Chinese girls because they're the only ones could make love properly."

"What do you think he meant by that, Unk?"

"I asked him and he claimed their vaginas are different, that they have a secret compartment women of other races don't. He said the Chinese leader Sun Yat-sen's wife, Soong Qingling, was famous for hers."

Roy was thirteen when he told this to his cousin Kip, Buck's son, who was four years older. Kip laughed and said, "My dad was joking."

"What if Mah Sam wasn't?" asked Roy.

MAH SAM

To Beat the Devil

After Roy's grandfather, whom he called Pops, died, Roy's mother's brother, Buck, came north from Florida to Chicago to bury the body. This was in February of 1960, two-day-old dirty snow was piled against the curbs and sidewalks were coated with ice. Pops had been living in a Florida nursing home for a few months prior to his fatal heart attack. Buck had moved his father to Tampa, where he lived with his wife and daughter, with the intention of having Pops live with them, away from the cold weather, but it had been necessary to instead place Pops in an assisted living facility where he could have on-site medical care. Pops had not wanted to leave Chicago, his home for sixty years, but he and his daughter did not get along, so Roy's uncle assumed responsibility for him.

Following his grandfather's funeral and burial, Roy, who was fourteen, accompanied his uncle around Chicago to say hello to former business associates of Buck's and to visit neighborhoods in which his uncle had built houses. Buck was a civil engineer and architect. He had relocated to Tampa two years before where there were more opportunities and fewer building restrictions. He also preferred being in warm weather year-round.

After cruising through the city and adjoining suburbs, Buck parked the car he'd borrowed from his sister in front of a one-story flat-roofed building with a sign on it that read DOMBROSKI & SON MACHINERY AND MANUFACTURING. It was only two-thirty in the afternoon but the sky was already dark and cloudy, threatening snow.

"Why are you stopping here, Unk?"

"There's a guy I want to see."

"Dombroski?"

"When I left Chicago he owed me some money. I heard he died. Maybe I can collect from his son."

"A lot of money?"

"Enough to give it a try."

"Can I come in with you? It'll be cold in the car."

"I'll leave the engine running with the heater on. This shouldn't take long."

Buck got out of the car and entered the building. Roy turned on the radio and listened to the news. Workers at a factory on the south side were on strike and someone got stabbed. The cops arrested two of the strikers and the victim was taken away in an ambulance. The White Sox had traded Chico Carrasquel, their shortstop, to the Cleveland Indians in order to make room for a top prospect, Luís Aparicio. Both players were from Venezuela. Snow was expected to begin falling on the city by four o'clock and continue throughout the night. People were advised to do their grocery shopping early, before the snow accumulated and made getting around difficult.

Roy turned off the radio. Flurries landed on the windshield. Roy had to pee, so he cut the ignition, put the key in a coat pocket, got out of the car, and ran around one side of the Dombroski building into the alley behind it. He urinated against the back wall, hoping nobody would see him. After Roy finished, he hurried back to the car. His uncle was standing next to the driver's side door. Buck's curly black hair was littered with white flakes.

"Sorry, Unk. I needed to pee bad."

He handed the car key to Buck.

"Did Dombroski's kid fork over what his old man owed?"

"Get in the car and I'll tell you."

Buck didn't say anything until he'd driven a couple of blocks. He turned on the windshield wipers.

"Turns out Dombroski was murdered a year ago. The business was in debt. His son, Buddy, declared bankruptcy. He gave me the phone number of the lawyer who's handling the claims. It doesn't matter, though, because his father and I never drew up a paper, it was a private matter."

"Who murdered him? Someone else he owed money to?"

"Buddy thinks the killer was the husband of a girl Dombroski was playing around with on the side."

"Is the husband in jail?"

"No. They can't prove he did it."

Snow was coming down harder, earlier than they said on the radio it would.

"Women and money, Roy, a man can't do without them, but there's always hell to pay."

"I once heard Pops say, 'Nobody beats the devil.' Is that what you mean?"

The snow came at them now from different angles, evading the swiping blades, clinging to the windshield.

"All I know, Roy, is that living is a very dangerous business."

The Man Who Swallowed the World

Sid Roman, Roy's mother's first cousin, was a kind, handsome, intelligent man who dropped his marbles at the age of forty-six. Cousin Sid, as Roy and his mother and her brother, Buck, always referred to him, worked for many years as a clothing salesman, specializing in men's suits, at one of Chicago's most exclusive and expensive haberdasheries. This mode of employment lasted, as Roy's mother phrased it, "until Cousin Sid lost his looks."

Actually, Cousin Sid's loss of his looks coincided with the loss of his mind. One day Sid could not find the silver cigarette lighter with his initials inscribed on it, a gift from his wife, Norma, for his fortieth birthday, and he decided that he had swallowed it. Cousin Norma was an equally kind, intelligent woman, who was "high strung" (again, Roy's mother's words), with a history of nervous breakdowns. Cousin Norma, an unhealthily thin woman with stringy red hair, who chain-smoked unfiltered Chesterfields, told her husband that he must simply have misplaced the lighter.

"Look in the pockets of your charcoal suit jacket," she told Sid. "It's in the pile to go to the dry cleaners."

"I already did," he answered, and pointed to his neck. "Look at my throat. There's where my lighter is, I can feel it."

"That's your Adam's apple," said his wife.

"I'm going to the emergency room," said Cousin Sid, "to have it removed."

He walked out of the house and did not return until six months later, when he was released from the psychiatric ward at Pafko Hospital.

After this, Cousin Sid behaved normally for a while; although, as Roy's mother observed, his looks were gone. Before his breakdown, he had resembled the actor William Powell, except for his hair, which Sid wore slicked back in the style of the day, and was silver and thicker than Powell's. During his residence at Pafko Hospital, however, Cousin Sid's teeth went bad, resulting in his having quite a large number of them removed. This gave him the appearance of his cheeks having caved in. Also, his color had changed: no longer glowing and golden, his face was now bloodlessly pale, bordering on unearthly. His mustache was gone, too, exposing a wrinkled and shrunken or shriveled upper lip that no longer covered completely his front teeth, of which one was missing. For some reason, he could not grow his mustache back, freezing his mouth in an expression somewhere between a sneer and a contemptuous grin.

Cousin Sid lost his job at the clothing store. Norma supported them and their fifteen-year-old son, Larry, who was disabled by polio and confined to a wheelchair, by working as a secretary for a law firm. It was months before Sid found work at a discount shoe

store on the south side of the city. The job required that he travel almost two hours on the elevated and two buses each way.

Four weeks after her husband began selling shoes, Norma received a call at the law office from the police informing her that Sid was in their custody at the Cottage Grove precinct. Sid had told a bus driver that he'd swallowed his transfer. When the driver ordered Sid to pay an additional fare, Sid refused, insisting that he was in possession of the transfer, it was in his stomach, and that he had also swallowed all of the money he'd had in his pockets so that it could not be stolen. The driver told him to get off the bus, but Sid took a seat and would not get up. The driver then radioed for the police, who came and removed him forcefully. Following this incident, Cousin Sid became convinced that he had swallowed everything from kitchen utensils to clocks, and Norma had him committed to an asylum in Indiana run by a nondenominational organization called Angels of Victims of Unfathomable Behavior.

Roy was nine when he accompanied his mother, Uncle Buck, and Cousin Norma to visit Cousin Sid in Indiana. It was a sunny, early October day, and Roy enjoyed riding in the backseat of his uncle's 1955 Cadillac Coupe Deville as they cruised through the Indiana dunes. Roy wondered how different they could be from the deserts of Egypt or Arabia, and imagined himself mounted on a camel among Bedouin tribesmen, his face shielded from blowing sand and intense sun by robes and gauzy scarves.

At the asylum, which was a huge black-and-gray stone building in the middle of nowhere that looked to him as if it should have been surrounded by a moat infested with crocodiles, Roy was made to sit alone in a waiting room while the others were taken by a woman wearing a gray nun's habit to see Cousin Sid. There was only one high window in the waiting room which admitted a narrow shaft of sunlight. It would be difficult to escape from this room, Roy thought, if the door were locked, especially because the six metal chairs were bolted to the floor and would have to be pried loose before they could be stacked high enough to reach the window. Roy remained there for an hour and was beginning to feel like the Count of Monte Cristo imprisoned in the Chateau d'If before the door opened and his Uncle Buck said, "Let's go, champ."

Seeing that his uncle was by himself, Roy asked, "Where are my mother and Cousin Norma?"

"Norma's pretty upset," said Buck. "Your mother is with her, taking a walk around the grounds."

Roy followed his uncle outside and they stood next to the Cadillac. Buck removed a cigar from an inside pocket of his navy blue sport coat, bit off one end, and felt in his other pockets for a book of matches.

"How's Cousin Sid?"

Buck located his matches and lit the cigar.

"He thinks he's swallowed everything he can't see."

"What do you mean everything? You mean including the Pacific Ocean and the Empire State Building?"

Buck took a few puffs. The smoke quickly disappeared into the crisp air.

"I suppose so," he said. "Whatever can't fit into his little room. I'm afraid it's the end of the world for Cousin Sid."

"He swallowed it," said Roy.

"What?"

"The world. He's got it all inside him."

Roy's mother and Cousin Norma came around the corner of the big, ugly building and walked slowly over to them. Cousin Norma was crying, a cigarette dangling from the left corner of her mouth. Her lips looked like two long crimson scratches. Roy's mother was holding Cousin Norma's right elbow. They all got into the car and nobody spoke until after Buck had been driving for fifteen minutes.

"I envy Sid," said Cousin Norma. "He doesn't have to think anymore."

"The sisters will take care of him," said Roy's mother; then she added, "I mean, the Angels."

"What's unfathomable behavior mean?" asked Roy.

"It's when somebody behaves in a way nobody else can understand," said his uncle.

Cousin Norma, who was sitting in the backseat with Roy, lit a fresh Chesterfield off a half-inch butt, which she then tossed out the window on her side. Her fingers were stained and wrinkled like a weathered, well-oiled baseball glove.

"Kitty," she said to Roy's mother, "I remember when I was about Roy's age, maybe a year younger, and my aunt gave me a beautiful girl doll for my birthday. I looked at it and then handed it back to her. My mother said, 'You can't do that, Norma. Take the doll and say thank you to Aunt Rose.' I ran away and locked myself in my room. I couldn't keep that doll, she was too beautiful and I was too ugly. I didn't want to have her around to haunt me, to constantly remind me of how I looked compared to her. I remember how I felt that day. It's the same way I feel now."

Roy stared out the window on his side at the sand dunes. He wanted to tell Cousin Norma the same thing he'd said to his uncle, that he thought Cousin Sid's world was inside him now, but he kept looking out the window and thought about the Arabs.

Evidence

Roy's father died in December of 1958, two months after Roy's twelfth birthday. His mother's third husband, Spanky Wankovsky, drove Roy to the wake, which was being held at the house his father had been living in with his second wife, Evie, and their son, Mickey, who was six years old. It was early afternoon when Roy arrived. The house was full of people, well-dressed men and women standing in the living and dining rooms and the kitchen, talking, drinking, and nibbling hors-d'oeuvres and slices of cake. The rooms were noisy and smoke filled from cigarettes and cigars. Evie, wearing a black dress and black hat with a veil, was the first to greet Roy. She was a kind and generous woman in her late twenties, twenty years younger than Roy and Mickey's father. A small woman, barely taller than Roy, Evie hugged him close to her body and said, "Oh, Roy, your father loved you so much, he didn't want to die. 'What will my boys do without me?' he said."

"Spanky dropped me off," Roy told her. "He'll bring my mother over later. And my Uncle Buck is in Florida."

"I know, Roy, he sent a telegram."

"Where's Mickey?"

"He's upstairs with his cousins, Jean and Diane. They'll come back down soon. There are many people here who want to see you."

For the next hour or more Roy accepted condolences from men and women, some of whom he knew, but most were strangers. All of them shook hands with Roy or put an arm around his shoulders while telling him what a good friend of theirs his father was, how important he'd been to their lives, how helpful he'd been, how irreplaceable, that it was terrible he died so young.

The mayor, too, had sent a telegram, which Roy's uncle Bruno, his father's older brother, read aloud. Several prominent politicians, including aldermen and judges, were present, Roy was told, as well as numerous business associates of his father's. Not a few of these people handed envelopes to Evie with instructions that their contents be divided equally between the sons.

Just as Mickey, Jean, and Diane came downstairs, Roy's mother arrived.

"Kitty's here!" exclaimed the two girls. "She's so glamorous!" said Diane, who was sixteen, a year older than her sister. "Stunning!" said Jean.

Kitty was wearing a full-length mink coat, her abundant auburn hair flowed down the sides of her head and rested on her shoulders, her full red lips shone like headlights. Like Evie, Kitty was much younger than Roy's father; she had turned thirty-two in November. As soon as she spotted Evie, Kitty rushed over to her and the two women embraced. Roy knew that his mother was sincerely fond of Evie, as was Evie of Kitty. Mickey stood next to Roy and held his hand.

Later that night at Roy's mother's house, Spanky Wankovsky, who was a jazz drummer, sat in a chair in the living room listening to a record. Roy came into the room and sat down on the piano bench. Spanky was thirty-eight and had been married to Kitty for almost two years. He and Roy did not get along well. At the wake, Spanky had stayed in the background, standing alone smoking cigarettes.

"Did you like my father?" Roy asked him.

Roy noticed that Spanky was keeping time to the music, tapping the fingers of his right hand on an arm of the chair.

"I didn't know him other than to say hello how are you. I knew what his business was, who many of his friends were. Your mother was afraid of them."

"Why? They wouldn't hurt her. They liked her."

"She's afraid of what they do, and what your dad did. Kitty is beautiful and polite to them, of course they dig her. Admire her, anyway. There were some dangerous men there today."

"What are you listening to?" Roy asked.

"Thelonious Monk and Johnny Griffin at the Five Spot in New York City. I went to hear them when they were here in Chicago a couple of months ago. This track is called 'Evidence.' "

"My dad never yelled at me or my brother, he never hit us. Uncle Buck liked him."

"He respected him, Roy. Respect and like are different things."

Roy stood up. "You don't know anything about my father," he said, then left the room.

Acapulco

Roy was eight years old when he and his Uncle Buck, his mother's brother, flew from Chicago to Mexico City. They were going to visit Buck's former father-in-law, Doc Wurtzel, at his house in Cuernavaca. Roy's cousin Kip, Buck's son by his first wife, Doc's daughter Juliet, had been living with his grandfather and his housekeeper, Pilar, for the past ten months, ever since his parents divorced. Kip was twelve now, and neither Roy nor Buck had seen him for a year. Juliet had had a nervous breakdown before the divorce, and Buck traveled often for his work as a structural engineer, mainly as a consultant on designing or reinforcing bridges, so Doc suggested that until a more suitable situation could be arranged, Kip come to live with him at his villa. Doc Wurtzel was a widower, a retired mineralogist; he and Buck had much in common and were fond of one another. It would be beneficial, both men agreed, for Kip to learn Spanish and to be away from his mother, whose instability prevented her from paying proper attention to her son. Buck told Doc he thought the best solution would be for Kip to be sent when he turned thirteen to a military academy; until then, Doc could provide the boy with valuable life experience.

It was January of 1954 when Roy and his uncle left freezing cold Chicago for sunny Mexico. Roy had been to Cuba, where his father had business, he spoke a little Spanish, and he looked forward to being in another Latin American country. Despite the four-year difference in their ages, Kip and Roy had always gotten

Doc Wurtzel

along well, as had Roy's mother, Kitty, and Juliet. Both women were beautiful and smart, said Buck, but troubled.

"Your mother and Kip's mother aren't really suited to raising children," Buck told Roy on the plane. "They're too self-absorbed to be responsible for others. Kip is better off for now with his grandfather and you with your father."

"What are we going to do at Doc's?"

"We'll stay at his place in Cuernavaca for a couple of days, it's not far from Mexico City; he's got a beautiful swimming pool lined with big white rocks, surrounded by flamboyana trees. I designed his patio and helped him build the pool. Then the four of us will drive cross country to Puerto Vallarta and go fishing. Doc has a special place he likes to hunt for marlin. After that maybe we'll stop over in Acapulco for a day or two."

"My mom and dad went to Acapulco on their honeymoon, I've seen pictures of them there."

"We'll rough it most of the way. Your dad tells me you're a good traveler."

"We once drove to Oriente from Havana, a lot of the way over mountains. It was kind of spooky sometimes. My dad kept a gun on the front seat between us, a .38. He showed me how to hold it with both hands and aim just below the target before I pulled the trigger."

"Did you have to shoot anybody?"

"No. Dad said there were bandits in the hills but all of the people we met were very nice. They were mostly black on that side of the island, different from in Havana. There are lots of pretty girls there."

Buck laughed and said, "There are pretty girls everywhere, Roy."

Doc's house was simply furnished and comfortable, with rattan chairs big enough for two people to sit in at the same time, and lots of doors to the outside that were always left open. Roy and Kip were happy to see each other again and Doc was a friendly, large man with a white beard and big hands. Kip told Roy that his grandfather could fix or build anything and that he was a championship fisherman. Pilar, Doc's live-in housekeeper, was a short, stout young woman with very long, shiny black hair.

"Pilar grew up in a small village near here," said Kip. "She's never even been to Mexico City and doesn't speak English. She doesn't speak good Spanish, either, mostly a local lingo Doc has trouble understanding. She's twenty-four. Doc sleeps with her sometimes, he says he does it to keep her happy because she's never been married and doesn't have any boyfriends."

"What if she gets pregnant?"

"I don't know. I guess the kid would live here with us. Pilar's parents never leave the village. Her sister, Tentación, comes to see her sometimes. She's only eighteen and has two kids already, a boy and a girl. Her husband, Pablo, breaks horses for ranchers around here. I've only met him once. He's shorter than I am but Doc says he knows how to sit a horse better than any man he's ever seen. Tentación told me Pablo's busted every bone in his body at least once."

"What does Tentación mean?"

"Temptation."

Doc and Buck sat and talked for two days, then the four of them loaded fishing and camping gear into the back of Doc's station wagon and headed for the west coast. The trip was uneventful but Roy enjoyed seeing what Mexico looked like. The country they drove through was not as verdant as Cuba; Doc said you had to go further south, to the state of Chiapas, to get into the forest.

"There's some serious jungle down that way," Doc said. "The Lacandon Indians live there and keep pretty much to themselves. They don't welcome outsiders. I hear they're tough folks to tangle with."

The men traded off driving and Roy got a little nervous when Doc drove because he sipped tequila all the time, but Kip told Roy Doc's secret to staying sober was to suck on venenoso limes while he drank. After a while Roy believed him because Doc was always steady on his feet and handled his customized, reinforced steel-bellied Willys expertly over bad roads.

"What's in the limes that keep him from getting drunk?" Roy asked Kip.

"Poison. That's what venenoso means."

The fishing at Puerto Vallarta wasn't so good. The marlin weren't running because of what Doc said was an unexpected cold spell, but he and Buck didn't seem to mind. All of the roads around the town were unpaved and the good weather didn't hold. Rather than camp out they stayed at a guest house that wasn't much more than a glorified lean-to. Kip taught Roy how to carve a resortera, a slingshot, out of a tree branch and they used stones to kill lizards. After three days of windy, wet weather and bad luck hunting marlin, Doc declared they should pack it in and make for Acapulco. There was a casino there, he said, and good restaurants.

In Acapulco, Doc decided they should check into a good hotel and clean up, then find the best place in town for martinis and steaks. After dinner, Kip and Roy walked with the men to a building next to the ocean with lots of steps leading up to the entrance.

"You boys wait here," Buck ordered when they were halfway up the steps. "Doc and I will be back in a little while."

The men continued up to the front door and Kip and Roy sat down on the steps and looked out at the Pacific. The sun was down but there was still a stripe of green light in the sky. The waves were gray-black and kicking up.

"Is this a casino?" Roy asked Kip.

"No, it's a prostíbulo, a whorehouse. They're going to get laid."

A few men went up and came down the steps while the boys sat there.

"Do you miss your mother?" Roy asked.

"Sometimes, but only when she's not drinking, and she was always drinking before I got shipped down here to Doc's. Does your mother drink?"

"No, not really. She says if she has more than one drink she falls asleep. She has other problems, though."

"Like what?"

"She faints a lot. Sometimes she screams for no good reason and her body shakes. My grandmother gives her pills and puts her to bed."

"Remember that time she showed us how to play craps on the sidewalk in front of my house and my mother came out and yelled at her and made me go inside? Your mother just laughed and picked up the dice then got into her car and drove away."

"Her maroon Roadmaster convertible."

"Yeah. Doc says she's as beautiful as Gene Tierney, maybe even more beautiful."

"Who's Gene Tierney?"

"Doc's favorite movie star ever since he saw her in *The Return of Frank James*. He said she went crazy and got put into an insane asylum."

After about an hour Doc and Buck came out of the house and walked down to where the boys were sitting. Roy and Kip stood up.

"How'd it go, Doc?" Kip asked.

"We got out alive, that's good enough. Let's go to the casino, I'll teach you to play craps."

"We know how to play, Roy's mother taught us."

"Kitty's my kind of woman," Doc said. "Don't you think so, Buck?"

The boys followed Doc and Buck into the Casino Encanto.

"You fellas look around," said Doc. "Buck and I are going to make back our meal money at the blackjack table."

Kip and Roy toured the big room watching people gamble. The roulette table was the busiest.

"Almost every guy in here has a gun on his hip," Roy said.

"The women have pistols in their purses," said Kip.

A few minutes later four men wearing bandanna masks and holding revolvers in their hands burst into the casino. One of them was shouting words Roy did not understand. Several of the patrons pulled out their guns and began shooting at the intruders, all four of whom immediately fired back at them. Most of the women crouched down, though a couple of them removed handguns from their purses and let fly at the masked men. Kip and Roy hit the floor and covered their heads with their arms. The shooting did not last long. Thirty seconds after it stopped Kip got up on his knees and looked toward the entrance.

"Come on, cousin," he said, "I think two of the robbers are dead and the other two ran out."

Both boys stood up. Kip pointed at the blackjack table.

"Your uncle and Doc are okay."

Roy saw them standing next to each other holding bills in their hands. Many of the gamblers were still hunkered down behind the tables or flat on the floor.

Later, when Buck, Doc, Kip, and Roy were on the street in front of the casino, Doc said, "Well, Roy, is life in Mexico exciting enough for you?"

"People get shot and killed in Chicago, too," said Roy.

That night, when they were alone in their hotel room, Roy asked Kip if he liked being in Mexico.

"Doc wants me to stay in Cuernavaca with him and go to school there. He knows I don't get along with my mother and that her new husband doesn't want me around. I guess I could get to like it here."

"Why did your mother marry a guy who isn't nice to you?"

"Doc says a lot of men, maybe women, too, don't like the idea of having another man's or woman's kid to raise."

"Why not go live with your dad?"

"Same reason. His wife is pregnant, she thinks I'll get in the way."

"Your father has something to say about it."

"If he does, he hasn't said anything to me."

Roy's parents had divorced when he was four years old and his mother had been married twice since then. Both marriages ended in divorce. She was single now.

"Maybe you could come to live with me and my mother. Do you want me to ask her?"

"I don't know. What if she gets married again and that guy don't go for me?"

"We'll run away together."

Kip laughed. "No, I'll stick with Doc; he gets lonely livin' with only his housekeeper. Besides, having two kids to handle would make it tougher for your mom to rope in husband number four."

"Boy, having kids can really mess things up," said Roy.

"I ain't never going to have any," said Kip.

At breakfast the next day Kip asked his grandfather, "Doc, if I stay with you, can Roy come, too?"

"It would be okay with me," said Doc, "but Roy's mother might object."

Doc looked at Roy, who smiled at him.

"Maybe not," said Roy.

When Roy got back to Chicago, his friend Jimmy Boyle asked him if he'd had a good time in Mexico. They were on their way home from school, walking against a strong wind that made their faces feel like apples being sliced into by paring knives.

"I don't know," said Roy. "I liked being with my Uncle Buck and being in better weather than this."

"Did anything bad happen?"

Roy didn't answer. He lowered his head, bent his body half over and thought about the gentle breezes that ruffled the leaves of the flamboyana trees around Doc Wurtzel's swimming pool.

When he and Jimmy got inside the front hall of Roy's house, Roy rubbed his face with his hands and said, "Nothing bad happened, it was only that I didn't feel like I belonged there."

"Do you feel like you belong here?" Jimmy asked.

Smart Guy

When Roy was twelve years old his mother told him a story about her brother, Buck, that her mother had told her.

"When your uncle was your age he got into real trouble. Buck was already making money from a company he created called Washtenaw Novelties. Nanny said that Buck found a way to buy up overstocked games and toys on the cheap from manufacturers and sold them at reduced prices by mail order. He advertised by taking out small ads in local newspapers. Buck has always been very smart when it comes to business."

"How did he get into trouble?"

"Some older boys convinced him to buy a car so that they could run away from Chicago. Buck was to go with them but he didn't know they were planning to kill him and bury his body in the woods. Your grandfather somehow found out about this plan, I think from the father of one of the boys, and told the police. Buck had already bought the car and driven off with the other boys. The police chased them down before they could dump my brother and got the boys to confess their plot."

"So Uncle Buck wasn't so smart, was he?"

"He got fooled, I guess."

"Did he or the other boys go to jail?"

"Nanny said the only crime any of them could be charged with was driving without a license. Buck had voluntarily given one of them who was old enough the money to buy it, so he couldn't be charged with anything. I believe they all got off."

"Did Uncle Buck tell Nanny and Pops why he wanted to run away?"

"My mother told me Buck just thought it would be an adventure. You know how he is, always ready to go somewhere and do something different."

"At least he's smarter now," said Roy.

His mother laughed. "In some ways," she said. "He's only in his forties and he's already been married and divorced three times."

Defining the Wind

Roy's Uncle Buck was the first person he knew who had a mobile phone in his car. This was in 1959, when only police and firefighters had telephone frequencies connected to their stations. Roy was with him when Buck bought a phone at a flea market in Tampa, Florida, installed it on the floor in front of the driver's side of his Cadillac Eldorado, and attached a maritime transmitter to tune in on a frequency for a marine operator. Roy did not understand exactly how Buck accomplished this but it worked.

One afternoon Roy, who was thirteen years old, was riding shotgun in the Eldo when his uncle, who was forty-five, decided to call an old girlfriend of his in Chicago.

"You mean you can call long distance from this phone?"

"Sure, I have it hooked up as if it was on the *Fujita*, my fishing boat. The marine switchboard doesn't know it's not."

"Why did you name your boat the *Fujita*?"

"A man named Fujita was a physicist at the University of Chicago who invented a tornado intensity scale. An F-1 has winds of seventy-three up to one hundred twelve miles per hour, an F-2 between one hundred thirteen and a hundred fifty-seven, and so on up to F-12, where winds can be as strong as seven hundred thirty-eight, the speed of sound."

"A boat probably couldn't stay afloat in an F-12, could it?"

"Certainly not, nephew. Not any craft smaller than an aircraft carrier. Even then the wind could create a whirlpool that would swallow the boat."

Buck called information in Chicago and asked if there was a listing for Francine Wayne. There was, so Buck asked to be connected to that number.

"How long has it been since you've spoken to her?" asked Roy.

"About ten years, since she got married. I heard she was divorced a couple of years ago and began using her maiden name again."

The phone rang several times before the operator came on the line to say there was no answer. Buck thanked her and hung up.

"Francine was a beautiful girl, Roy. She was working as a salesgirl at Marshall Field's department store on State Street when I met her at the perfume counter. I was buying a bottle of Chanel No. 5. Francine asked me who it was for and I told her, my mother, for her birthday, which was the next day. Francine said that was okay then. I said, I'm glad you approve. She gave me a little smile and said, I'm sure your girlfriend would have preferred a different scent. I asked her which perfume she favored. Francine told me and I asked her if the store carried it. She said yes and put a bottle on the counter. I told her to add it onto my bill for the Chanel. She did and I handed the bottle to her. For you, I said, and then I asked her out to dinner."

"Do you remember the name of that perfume?"

"No. Francine was a modest girl, serious, she rarely smiled. If I had to choose one word to describe her it would be demure. I never could tell if she was ever really happy. I'll try to call her again later."

"Have you been thinking about her lately?"

"I have. At about an F-2 level on the Fujita scale. I don't know why."

Francine

Crosses

When he was twelve years old Roy accompanied his Uncle Buck to the funeral service for Buck's longtime housekeeper, Fortune Chase, who had died a few days before. Fortune was only forty-six years old, two years younger than Roy's uncle, when she had a heart attack. She had worked for Buck for fifteen years. He and Roy were the only white people in the church.

"Fortune was always good to me, Unk. She made sure I had enough to eat and never got mad at me for anything. Did she have any kids?"

"Not that I know of. She had a husband for a while, Amos, but I haven't seen him in the last two or three years. He was usually in jail or out of work. I hired him once to lay sewer pipe but he disappeared after a few days. I told Fortune about it and she just said nobody was paying her to keep track of him."

Following the service at The Church of the Innocent Blood in West Tampa, Buck told Roy that they would not be going to the cemetery for Fortune's burial.

"Let's go to Las Novedades, in Ybor City. You like their Cuban sandwiches."

"Okay, Unk. That's the first time I've ever been in a black church."

"How did you like it?"

"I liked that all of the women were wearing long white dresses, even Fortune in her coffin, and I liked the music. I didn't understand all of what the preacher woman was saying, though."

"What didn't you understand?"

"What did she mean when she said that she was done packing her crosses?"

"She was speaking for Fortune, Roy, not herself. It was a way of saying that Fortune was finished with this life, that her business on earth was done. In the hereafter Fortune will no longer have any crosses to bear."

"How does she know?"

"Nobody knows, Roy, but it makes some people feel better to believe it."

"You don't, do you, Unk?"

"No. Sometimes I wish I could."

The drive from West Tampa to Ybor City took about twenty minutes. Roy did not ask his uncle any more questions.

Good Kids

Erskine Copperhead's personalized license plate on his 1960 Chevy pickup read LRDA MCY. One time when he was paused at a STOP sign, a pedestrian crossing the street in front of his truck pointed at the plate, shouted, "Can't you spell?" and walked on. Erskine did not bother to tell the spelling expert that a maximum of eight letters were allowed on license plates in the state of Florida. Perhaps the convict at Apalachee or Okeechobee or whichever correctional facility who stamped the plate also wrinkled his nose at the inadequate abbreviation, but if so his complaint never reached Erskine. Being a devout Baptist, he felt confident that like-minded individuals would nevertheless appreciate the advertised sentiment.

Erskine worked as a sewer repairman and installer for Hebrew County. He was thirty-seven years old, unmarried, had most of his own teeth, and prided himself that he was modest in his needs. Work, church on Sundays, no more than two beers a day, clean sheets once a month. That about covered it for Copperhead, except for one thing: he craved the company of adolescent boys. Erskine longed for the days of his boyhood, when he and his buddies went swimming and fishing together in the Big Two-Headed Hebrew River, roughhoused, played baseball, and knew not what changes were in store for them once they assumed adulthood.

His encounter with Roy and Sparky occurred on a sweltering Sunday afternoon when Erskine was returning home following services at Eulalia Love's Face of Grace Baptist Church. Before picking up an order of spare ribs at Alabama John's Barbecue, Copperhead stopped at a Li'l General convenience store to buy a carton of Marlboros. He was standing in line for the register when he overheard the two boys behind him discussing which brand of beer to purchase. Erskine turned to look at them.

"How old are you fellas?"

"How old are you?" asked Roy.

"Thirty-seven, unless my mama been lyin' to me."

"I'm thirteen," Sparky said. "Roy's twelve and a half."

"You expectin' the clerk here to sell you an alcoholic beverage?"

"No, expect you to buy it for us. We give you the price and some extra."

"What's your name, son?"

"Sparky Duda. What's yours?"

"Erskine Copperhead. Sparky and Roy, huh? You live hereabouts?"

"Next thing he'll want to know if our parents know we're fixin' to break the law."

"River Grove," said Sparky. "Roy's down from Chicago, visiting his uncle."

"Used to I'd go skinny dippin' in the Hebrew River. Bet you boys do, too."

"You like watchin' naked boys swim?" asked Roy.

"Next!" said the clerk.

Sparky shoved a six-pack of canned Budweiser into Copperhead's hands. Roy put a five-dollar bill on top of it. Erskine put the six-pack and the carton of Marlboros on the counter.

"That be all?" the clerk asked.

Erskine looked at him.

"You ain't from here. Where you from?"

The clerk was bald except for patches of fuzzy black hair above each ear, had a thick, waxed mustache twirled at the ends; his skin was dark brown.

"I am a citizen of the United States of America, sir. Are you?"

"Lorda mercy," said Copperhead. "Ask a question around here, get one right back."

The clerk lifted the fin off the six-pack, deposited it in the cash register, and handed two quarters to Erskine.

Sparky and Roy followed him out of the store. Once they were on the sidewalk, Sparky tugged at the six-pack.

"Let go. You got our money."

Erskine loosened his grip and Sparky took the beer.

"I could be arrested, doin' you a charity. Throwed in jail."

"You'd do less time than you get caught pinchin' little boys' weenies," said Roy.

"This your truck?" asked Sparky.

"It are."

"What's that written on the license plate supposed to mean?"

"World's full of surprises, many not real agreeable. Man alone's in need of God's helpin' hand."

A black and light-blue Hebrew County Sheriff's Department car drove up and parked alongside Erskine's pickup. A uniformed deputy got out and looked at Sparky holding the six-pack.

"Afternoon, officer," Sparky said, "hot as blazes, isn't it?"

He removed a can and handed it to the deputy.

"Straight out the cooler."

The deputy grinned, popped the top, looked at Erskine Copperhead and said, "Real good kids we got around here."

La Recompensa

"Why can't you go back to Vera Cruz, Unk?"

"Not can't, Roy, won't."

"Did something bad happen to you there?"

"Yes, but something worse will happen if I go back."

Roy, who was twelve years old, and his Uncle Buck were on Buck's boat, *Trópico*, in the Gulf fishing for grouper. So far the only fish that had taken the bait were sharks.

"Was it because of a married woman?"

Buck laughed. "What else?"

"How would her husband know you were there?"

"The only reason I would be there would be for María. Besides, there's una recompensa out for whoever turns me in."

"What's that?"

"A reward. Her husband is a rich bandit who put a price on my head. He also told his wife that if she ever saw me again he'd have her killed, too."

"Maybe he's forgotten about you, or she has."

"In Mexico, nobody forgets."

"I've got a bite, Unk."

"So does María."

BANDIDO

The Golden Ball

Buck knew Gina was no good but he enjoyed her company. She was thirty-five years younger than he—twenty-three—an accommodating sex partner, and presentable enough to take to a restaurant. Gina had grown up poor in Port St. Joe, Florida, and come to Tampa, where Buck lived, to see if she could get by on her looks. Gina was a soft hooker, mostly hustling older men for meals, rent money, ready cash and occasionally getting a trip to the Bahamas or Atlanta, where one of the men she dated got her hired to perform in a pornographic movie. Gina liked the fact that she was paid five hundred dollars for an afternoon's work being filmed performing oral sex on several men, but she decided not to pursue this as a profession. The other girls in the movie were either drug addicts or alcoholics or working their way through college; some hoped to go to Hollywood and become legitimate actresses. Gina decided to stick to keeping company with one or two men at a time for so long as he paid her bills, put something in her pocket on a regular basis, and wasn't too demanding.

Buck would occasionally buy gold necklaces, bracelets, and rings from a second-story man named Larry Boyd and then melt them down to form a ball of solid gold. He had a workshop in his house that he used for his alchemical and other projects which he kept locked at all times. He made the mistake of one day showing to Gina his ball of gold, which was the size of a baseball. He told her its value was in the thousands of dollars.

LARRY BOYD

The next night two men broke into the house, hit Buck on the head with a short length of pipe, knocked down the door to his workshop, and ransacked the room until they found the golden ball. They took that along with various tools and left Buck unconscious on the floor of his bedroom.

After he recovered, Buck did not call the police. Instead he bought several guns which he loaded and placed strategically throughout his house. He knew that Gina had any number of shady, if not criminal, acquaintances to one or more of whom she might have divulged the existence and precise location of his ball. He then contacted his pal Larry Boyd, gave him a couple of hundred dollars, and told him to ask around to find out who the perpetrators were.

A week later, Larry came to Buck's house and told him he was pretty sure who the thieves were and asked Buck if he wanted him to do something about it. Buck gave Larry a cold piece, a thirty-eight caliber revolver he'd bought from an ex-cop, and told him to see if he could get the golden ball back and if necessary to shoot the thieves and ditch the gun in Tampa Bay. He promised to pay Larry a thousand dollars if he retrieved the ball. Boyd asked Buck what he should do if they'd already sold the ball and Buck said to shoot them anyway.

As it turned out, when Larry confronted one of the thieves it was Larry who got shot in his right leg. When he was able to walk again, he came to see Buck, told him he did not get the ball, and that as far as he knew both of the guys had left town. Buck paid Larry's medical expenses, gave him seven hundred dollars, and told him to not come around for a while. Buck reminded him to deep-six the thirty-eight if he had not already done so.

The next time Gina called Buck he told her he never wanted to see her again. She did not ask him why.

A Chicago Girl

Roy and his Uncle Buck stayed up late one night watching a movie on television, a western about a young gunslinger named Kid Deadeye who in the 1890s avenges his brother's killing by the Dime-a-Dozen Gang in South Texas and Old Mexico. After the movie was over, Buck told his nephew that he had known one of the actresses in it.

"Which one?" asked Roy.

"The half-Mex whore who shoots the man who'd abused her by putting a double-barreled shotgun into his open mouth and pulling both triggers while he's sleeping."

"That's one of the best scenes in the movie, Unk. How did you know her?"

"After the war, in 1948, I worked as an engineer for the city of Van Nuys. I lived in Los Angeles, in West Hollywood. I met Pearl Roland at a party. She was just getting started as an actress, she was twenty-two, fifteen years younger than I. She'd come to the party with the actor Robert Taylor, who was married to Barbara Stanwyck, who had been famous for more than twenty years. I didn't know if Pearl and Taylor were having an affair or not, it was none of my business, but I couldn't resist making an attempt to get to know her."

"Did you and she become friends?"

"No, Roy, I never met her again after that night. We talked about Chicago, where both of us had grown up. Pearl mostly had

Pearl Roland

small roles in movies, a few of which I went to see because she was in them. She was always the prettiest girl and a good enough actress but never the leading lady, except in a couple of low-budget black-and-white B movies. In *Never for Love* she played a young woman who married one much older man after another, each of whom died soon thereafter, leaving her their money. Pearl was a brunette with green cat's eyes, a slightly turned down mouth with full lips, a drawn-on birthmark on her left cheek, and a long narrow nose with wide nostrils. I've never seen another face like hers."

"What happened to her, Unk?"

"I followed her career for a while, but three or four years after we met, Pearl Roland was in a well-publicized automobile accident. Her male companion, who was driving, a prominent actor at the time whose name I've forgotten, was killed. Pearl's nose was severed by the rearview mirror. I was living back in Chicago when I read about it."

"I guess that was the end of her movie career."

"Apparently she had several plastic surgeries to rebuild her nose. I saw Pearl in one movie when she was in her early thirties, a horror film made in France called *The Beast that Ate Montmartre*, some silly title like that. Her face wasn't the same."

"How did she look?"

"All right. She was only in a few scenes, she still had a birthmark on her left cheek."

Women and Fish

It was the last day of June and the sun was on its way down when Roy's Uncle Buck hooked a black marlin. They were out in the Gulf Stream in Buck's powerboat, the *Corazón*, just the two of them. Roy was eleven years old and his uncle was forty; after a long day in the sun they had not had a big strike and were ready to head back to Tampa when Buck said, "I'll leave a line out to troll, go slow, maybe we'll get a hit."

Roy's uncle grabbed his rod and checked the drag. Just then a fish struck.

"It feels like a black!" he said.

"How can you tell?"

"Heavy, heavier than a striped, sinks right away, heads for the bottom. A striped'll run right out, jump sooner and fight longer, but for the first forty minutes, maybe a little more, a black sinks like a boulder barreling down the side of a mountain. You can't stop him any more than you can stop an avalanche."

Roy helped strap his uncle into a fighting chair then took the wheel again.

"Tell me when you need water, Unk," he said.

The marlin ran for almost an hour before Buck felt the line go slack.

"Keep her slow and steady, Roy. Head for the cut to the bay. West northwest."

Buck reeled steadily, the sun was on the lip of the horizon and Roy kept an eye out for the cut, hoping there would be enough light left for him to take the boat through. He flipped on the running lights just as the marlin leapt out of the water and smacked back down sideways.

"Look, Roy! It's a big black! He's tired. I told you he wasn't going to last long. Let her idle and get the gaff."

Before Roy could move, Buck shouted, "He's diving again!"

The line snapped and the fish was gone.

"My fault," said Buck, "the line was too taut."

He reeled in what was left of it, unstrapped himself, and opened a bottle of beer.

"Do you see the cut yet?"

"Just ahead, Unk."

That night Buck and Roy picked up Buck's girlfriend Loretta Vampa and drove to Bob's Lobster Pot.

"I understand you and your uncle didn't have much luck today," she said.

"The unk hooked a black marlin but it got away. Did you ever read that story *The Old Man and the Sea*?"

"No. Did the old man hook a marlin and lose him?"

"He didn't lose his fish but sharks ate most of it before he could bring it to shore."

"Do you want to be a civil engineer like your uncle?"

"He wants to be a writer," said Buck.

"I read a little," Loretta said, "but not enough to hurt me."

Loretta was twenty years younger than Roy's uncle. She worked as a hairdresser.

"The last time I saw you," said Roy, "you were a blonde. Now you're a redhead."

Loretta fluffed her hair with both hands.

"Do you like it, Roy? Do you think I rate better as Marilyn Monroe or Rita Hayworth?"

"Tell her she should go back to her natural color," said Buck.

"I'm thinking about going to college," Loretta said.

"You'll have to read there," said Roy. "It might hurt."

Not for Everyone

Alfonso Sola was a happy man. In his mid-twenties, he worked as a ferryboat operator in Havana, Cuba, between the mainland and a nearby island. Alfonso was a handsome, sweet-natured guy, not well educated but obviously intelligent. He was one of the few residents of Cuba in the 1980s who was satisfied with his life, though he was not a particular admirer of Fidel Castro. His satisfaction stemmed from the fact that he had a decent job and was happily married to a woman with whom he had two young children. Alfonso also had a mistress in Havana with whom he had one child. Due to his schedule on the ferryboat, Alfonso was able to split his time and affections between his two families.

His *compadres*, many of whom rode on the ferry to and from their jobs, knew about his double life and, charmed as they were by him, could only admire Alfonso's *machismo*. Despite the dire Cuban economic situation, Alfonso managed to create a good life for himself. He was one person who did not want to leave Cuba. A number of his friends, however, were desperate to escape to the United States, and they attempted to convince him to leave with them, entreaties which Alfonso rejected. He wished them well but was determined to remain.

The day came when a group of his friends decided to hijack Alfonso's ferryboat and flee to Key West, Florida. Alfonso attempted to prevent them from seizing control of the boat but they subdued him, all the while trying to convince Alfonso that it would be best for him to go, too. His friends forcibly restrained him and when the boat arrived in Key West the fugitives were taken by harbor authorities to a detention center and given political asylum. Alfonso tried to tell the US immigration agents that he did not want to stay in the United States, that he had been hijacked and taken to Florida against his will. Since he spoke very little English, it was difficult for him to communicate with certain of the government people and he was put on a bus with the others to Miami.

In Miami, many of his fellow immigrants were taken in by relatives already living there. Alfonso reluctantly went with one of them knowing that if he returned to Cuba the government there would most likely not believe his story and treat him as a criminal. He was afraid that he might be imprisoned or even shot as a traitor. Alfonso retained his charm, however; people invariably liked him, especially women. He soon met a young woman who showed him around Miami, introducing him to a life of plenty—to Alfonso's eyes—that he could not have imagined. Alfonso and the girl had a romance but he was not really happy. They moved to Tampa, where his girlfriend had family, and he found a job as a waiter in a restaurant. Alfonso longed for his life on the water driving the ferryboat. He missed his wife, his mistress, his children. Finally he told the girl that he had to return to Cuba, that he could talk his way out of his situation. Why would he go back, he'd say, unless his story was true? Certainly, Alfonso convinced himself, the Cuban authorities would believe him. He took a bus to Miami and in Coral Gables stole a small powerboat and took off for Cuba. As Alfonso headed home, passing in the opposite direction was an overcrowded boat filled with fleeing would-be immigrants, on its way to Florida. Among the passengers were Alfonso's wife and children as well as his former mistress and child. As the boats passed each other, Alfonso waved and the freedom seekers waved back.

Two years later, Buck Colby, an American who had befriended Alfonso in Tampa, ran into him at the Floridita Bar in Havana. He told Buck about his miraculous return to Cuba and that he had recognized both his wife and mistress clinging to the railing of the boat he had passed. Alfonso now had a new wife and a new mistress and said he was working again on a ferryboat. He was *contento*, he said, and that America is not for everyone.

A Day on the Lake

In 1934, when he was twenty-three years old, Buck Colby went sailing with his engineering classmate at the University of Illinois, Dusty Fenimore, on Dusty's family's ketch, the *Friendship*. Accompanying the two men were nineteen-year-old twin sisters from Chicago named Azimuth and Vega Rivers. Both men were experienced sailors—Buck went on to become a lieutenant commander in the United States Navy—and they skillfully maneuvered the *Friendship* from its berth at the Columbia Yacht Club in Chicago onto Lake Michigan. It was on a Saturday afternoon, a mild, sunny day in mid-July. Neither of the girls had been sailing before; they were eager to be on the water with Dusty, an acquaintance of Azimuth's, and Buck, whom they did not meet until that morning.

The *Friendship* set sail shortly after noon. Their plan was to spend four or five hours sailing. The girls had packed a lunch for the four of them. The story of what happened that day was not revealed to Buck until many years later. All he knew was that neither of the men ever met with the young women again. Twenty-five years later Vega was believed to have been murdered in her apartment on Orchard Street on the near north side of the city by an unknown assailant. Buck, who had established a construction firm in Chicago, read about the killing in the *Tribune* and telephoned Dusty, who lived and worked in New York City.

"What about Azimuth?" Dusty asked him. "Have you heard anything from or about her?"

Buck told him he had not and that he didn't know if she were still living in Chicago. Neither Buck nor Dusty mentioned their day on the lake with the sisters.

"I just thought you'd like to know about this," Buck said.

"Yes, it's terrible. I've never forgotten Vega and Azimuth."

Three months after his brief conversation with Dusty, Buck received a letter from Azimuth addressed to him at his office.

Dear Buck,

I hope you remember me. You and your friend Dusty Fenimore took my sister Vega and myself sailing one afternoon on his boat on Lake Michigan more than twenty years ago. Perhaps you've read or heard on the news that Vega was found dead in her apartment in Chicago recently. At first the police thought that she had been murdered but now it's been determined that she committed suicide. The details don't matter. All that matters is that my sister is dead. I'm writing to you now to tell you the possible reason. It involves Dusty. That day on the boat while you and I were sitting together in the stern and you were showing me how to handle the tiller, Dusty and Vega were below deck having sex. Did Dusty tell you? Vega did not tell me until that night. She said it happened quickly, that Dusty assaulted her and afterwards Vega was too ashamed to say anything. I believe that she was in shock. You may recall that she barely spoke for the rest of the afternoon. Anyway, she became pregnant. Dusty was only the second man she had had sex with. Vega never told him. When her pregnancy became obvious she went to Ft. Lauderdale, Florida, where the baby was born in a Catholic home for unwed mothers. Vega gave up the child for adoption, she never saw it. After a couple of months she returned to Chicago and lived with me until I got married two years later. Vega suffered from chronic depression for the rest of her life. Therapy did not help her. She never had a successful relationship with a man and lived alone until she died. Vega was not the same person after that day on the lake. I have not attempted to contact Dusty Fenimore nor do I intend to. If you are in touch with him and choose to tell him about Vega I do not wish to know. I have told you because you were very nice to me that afternoon. I still remember your kindness and patience when you were instructing me how to work the tiller. I've never gone sailing again.

Yours, Azimuth
(Mrs. Robert Remington)

Dusty had never told Buck about his having had a dalliance with Vega. He looked up Robert Remington in the Chicago telephone directory, then called the number. A woman answered.

"May I speak to Mrs. Remington, please. Azimuth Rivers Remington."

"Who's calling?"

"Buck Colby. I'm an old acquaintance of hers."

"What do you wish to speak to her about?"

"Her sister, Vega."

"This is she. Hello, Buck."

"Hello, Azimuth. I received your letter today."

"I assume you were surprised."

"Yes. I'm sorry about Vega. I'd like to ask you a question."

"All right."

"Are you certain that Dusty was the father of her child?"

"I am."

"Wasn't it really your child, Azimuth? I recall that you and Dusty had a relationship prior to that day the four of us spent together on the lake."

Azimuth hesitated before saying, "How did you know?"

"I didn't."

Azimuth hung up.

When Buck told this story to his wife, she asked, "Why would Azimuth send you a letter? And why would she lie about the child being Vega's?"

"They were twins," said Buck. "Identical twins. They often think alike."

"But one of them is dead."

"Yes, that's what I mean. What difference does it make?"

A year or so later, Buck was in New York City, where he met with Dusty Fenimore. They had dinner together, talking about old times and catching up on their current activities. Dusty asked Buck if he had heard again from Azimuth and Buck related to him the conversation he'd had with her.

Dusty did not say anything for thirty seconds. Finally, he said, "Azimuth was a strange girl when I knew her. She refused to see or even speak to me after we went sailing that day. I had no idea why. We'd never had an argument. I believe we slept together two or three times, but it was casual, pleasant rather than passionate. That was it. I don't really know what to make of what she told you, or even your take on the situation. You might be right, of course. It's a mystery, and I think we should leave it that way. As Jean Renoir said in his film *The Rules of the Game*, the terrible thing is that everyone has his reasons. Azimuth has hers."

Mombasa

When Buck was forty-one years old, soon after he had opened his civil engineering office in Chicago, he received an air letter in care of his mother from Karl Adlig, a friend from his undergraduate days at the University of Alabama. The thin light-blue envelope was postmarked Mombasa, Kenya, and dated May 9, 1952, the day after Buck's birthday.

"Hello, old pal, I bet you're surprised to hear from me after so many years. I still have your family's home address in Chi so I hope this gets to you, wherever you are. Last I knew you were with the OSS, stationed in London—then Ireland, I think—before the war, fourteen or fifteen years ago. I thought of you yesterday and remembered that it was your birthday! So just wanted to say Happy Birthday and let you know that I'm still breathing and mostly in one piece. The Krauts got me in my right kneecap—I was in the infantry—shattered it and made sure I would limp like a trampled on bull or bronc rodeo rider for the rest of my life—but it got me out of the army. Anyway, I'm in Africa now, in Mombasa, Kenya. In some ways it reminds me of Mobile, where I grew up. You went home with me there once, didn't you? For Thanksgiving one year. Not much space to scribble on this aerogram so I'll fill you in on what I'm doing here. I went to work in

the coffee business in New Orleans after I was discharged. No jobs to be had in Alabama, and after a while was sent to Kenya to work in the office here in Mombasa to learn the bean end of things. Since I'm a southern boy they figured I could handle the heat. I have an office looking out over the water. It's about the end of the rainy season. I took up with a local gal, her name is Cleopatra Ngongo, a chief's daughter, she claims. All the girls here are chief's daughters! Coal black, of course, and beautiful. I feel like Rhett Butler who's gone over. She's twenty-two years old and pregnant. We're married. She has a twenty year old sister named Helen-of-Troy—I kid you not—who is even more beautiful than Cleo. Why don't you come over and meet her? You were always a ladies' man, you handsome devil, she'll eat you up, but if you mistreat her she'll just eat you! Joking of course. These girls have had a British education, they speak more proper English than I do. I might could even get you a job with the Royal Blend Coffee Company. About out of writing room, have to quit. Would like to know what you're doing. Write me care of Royal Blend, Mombasa, Kenya, British East Africa. Roll Tide! Karl"

Buck recalled the time he accompanied Karl from Tuscaloosa to Mobile for Thanksgiving. He'd watched Karl's mother chop off a turkey's head with a hatchet she said Karl had made when he was thirteen, pluck and clean the bird, and dress it. Karl's father and younger brother, Hermie, roasted it over a pit in their yard. Buck could not picture their visiting Karl in

Mombasa or his bringing Cleopatra to Alabama. She and Helen-of-Troy probably were really beautiful, though.

The German Officer

It was Roy's friend Sparky Duda who first asked Roy's Uncle Buck if he had ever killed anyone.

"You were a spy in Europe before the war and later in action in the navy. You were in the South Pacific, weren't you?"

"I was," said Buck.

"Did you have to kill anyone, Unk? I mean face-to-face, not firing a big gun from a ship."

Both Roy and Sparky were fourteen years old. They were on Buck's powerboat in the Gulf of Mexico fishing for yellowtail and grouper.

"I've got a bite, boys," Buck said. "Get the net, Roy."

Earlier that morning, when the three of them were loading rods and ice chests onto the boat, Buck had talked about the time he'd spent in Ireland in the 1930s, when he'd been an agent for the Office of Strategic Services.

"I still have a pistol I got there, a Mauser Broomhandle C96. All the German officers carried one."

"What were Germans doing in Ireland?" asked Sparky.

"Before the war started people in Northern Ireland were inclined to side with Germany against the British. I was embedded there to find out just how favorably disposed they were."

"How did you get that gun, Unk?"

Buck reeled in a small yellowtail, took it off the hook, and threw it back into the water.

"I took it off a guy."

"Did you have to kill him to get it?" Sparky asked. "Did he draw on you?"

Buck put fresh bait on his hook and cast it out.

"Yes," he said.

Later that afternoon, when the boys were back at Sparky's house in Tampa, Sparky asked Roy, "Do you think your uncle will tell me the rest of the story?"

"If he wanted to he would have already told us."

The next day Roy asked his uncle, "Did you know him?"

"Know who?"

"The man you killed. Was he a German officer?"

"His name was Dieter Sehr. We lived in the same rooming house in Derry. He was half-blind, he told me he'd lost his left eye in a saber duel."

"Why did you have to kill him? Was he a spy, too?"

"He was gathering information to determine how and where the German army could land their troops. I'll show you his Mauser sometime if you want to see it."

The German Officer

Where the Dead Hide

"Look in the bottom drawer of the dresser in the dining room, Roy. The placemats are underneath a burgundy tablecloth."

Roy's mother was having a dinner party that night and Roy, who was fourteen, was helping her prepare the table. He knelt down and felt around under the tablecloth and found the placemats, which he took out, as well as a thick piece of paper that was partially stuck to the underside of the placemat on the bottom. He carefully separated the paper from the placemat without tearing it and read what was printed on it.

"Hey, Ma, who is James O'Connor?"

His mother walked from the kitchen into the dining room and said, "Who?"

"I found this document in the bottom of the drawer. It's a marriage certificate with Nanny's name on it and a James O'Connor. I didn't know she'd been married to anyone other than Pops."

"Let me see it."

Roy handed her the certificate and stood up. His mother scanned it, then said, "Yes, Roy, she was, for about ten years, from the time I was six until I was sixteen."

"So she and Pops got divorced."

"Yes."

"Why didn't you ever tell me?"

"I didn't think it was important, I guess. O'Connor died when I was in my last year of high school, and Nanny died when you

James O'Connor

were eight, so I didn't really see the point. Also, since you and Pops are so close, I didn't want to say anything that might affect your relationship with him."

"So you really grew up with this guy O'Connor. He was your stepfather."

"Oh, I was away most of the time at boarding school, and then in the summer I went to Kansas City to visit my father, who was living there for much of the time Nanny and O'Connor were married."

"Did you live here then, in this house?"

"No, O'Connor had a house in Norwood Park, about thirty miles west of Chicago. After O'Connor died, my mother sold that house and we moved back into the city."

"Did Pops own this house?"

"Yes, he still does. Half of it, anyway. I own the other half."

Roy's mother rolled up the certificate and said, "I'll tie a ribbon around this."

"Why did you keep it?" Roy asked.

His mother looked at him but didn't say anything.

"What about Uncle Buck?"

"What about him?"

"Did he live in Norwood Park, too?"

"No, Roy, my brother is twelve years older than I am, he was already pretty much gone by the time Nanny married O'Connor. He was at the University of Alabama for a couple of years before he went into the navy."

"What about when he came back?"

"He and O'Connor didn't get along. I'm not sure why, but O'Connor didn't want Buck around, so he stayed with friends in Chicago. It was easier for him to find jobs in the city."

"I wonder why Uncle Buck never told me about Nanny being married to O'Connor."

"It was a difficult time for my brother. O'Connor wouldn't even let Buck see Nanny at their house. She used to meet him at restaurants and other places in Chicago. I guess it's painful for him to talk about that time."

"Did O'Connor like you?"

"He was always polite and nice enough, I suppose. I was just a little girl. As I said, I was off at a Catholic boarding school, so he didn't have to deal with me very much. My mother took care of me. Besides, O'Connor spent a lot of time with his brothers, they were in the warehouse business in the Chicago area and other cities in the Midwest. He was always busy or going out of town somewhere."

"Did you call him Dad?"

"No, Mr. O'Connor."

Roy's mother walked back into the kitchen. Rain began beating at the windows. Roy went into the living room and looked outside. The sky was darkening quickly and rain was hitting the windows harder in the front of the house. He thought about Pops living alone in a hotel in Chicago. Roy's Uncle Buck had recently moved to Florida and wanted Pops to live down there with him and his wife and daughter. Pops was almost eighty years old, the winters in Chicago were hard on him, so Roy figured it would be better for his grandfather to live somewhere warm. Roy loved Pops more than anyone else in his family. Pops was his best friend and Roy knew he would miss him a lot. James O'Connor didn't sound like he was such a good guy, especially his not having been kind to Buck, whom Roy loved almost as much as he loved Pops. Roy's father had been dead for two and a half years now. Maybe, Roy thought, he would go to Florida, too.

Buck's mother
ROSE

The Tongues of Dying Men

Roy's cousin Kip never forgave his parents for sending him at the age of thirteen to a military school in Indiana. It was during his second year there that his mother divorced his father and afterwards did everything she could to keep Kip away from him. Soon after the divorce his father moved from Chicago to Tampa, Florida, and did not see his son for the next four and a half years.

It was not until after Kip's third year at the University of Illinois that he drove down to Tampa to see his father again. By this time Kip's mother had remarried and become addicted to tranquilizers that slowly shredded her formerly sharp mind into fragments. His father was pleased to see him but both of them quickly came to realize that they had little in common. Their reunion lasted barely a month before Kip decided to return to Chicago. His father did not attempt to convince Kip to stay any longer, gave him money for food and gas, and let him go. They never saw each other again.

After graduating from college, Kip enlisted in the army and nine months later was sent to Vietnam, where he was killed during combat. His mother did not inform his father of Kip's death until more than a year later.

Before being shipped off to war, Kip wrote a letter to him that he never mailed. He put it into a drawer in a table next to the bed in his room at his mother and stepfather's house. She discovered this letter six months after he'd written it, read it, then tore it up. Two years later, alone and in a drug-induced delirium, she passed out after accidentally setting fire to the house and was incinerated. What was left of her body was buried next to Kip's.

Roy was four years younger than his cousin and had always looked up to him. The night before Kip was to leave for boot camp, he and Roy watched *The Treasure of the Sierra Madre* on television. At the end of the movie, when wind blows gold dust the two miners had worked for a year to acquire into their faces, men who do not yet realize that their labor and suffering has come to nothing, Kip said to Roy, "That's all we have to look forward to, cousin, spitting into the wind and having the wind spit it back."

The next morning, before Roy drove him to the train station, Kip handed him what he told Roy was his last three hundred dollars. Roy never forgot this and that his cousin was smiling when he said it.

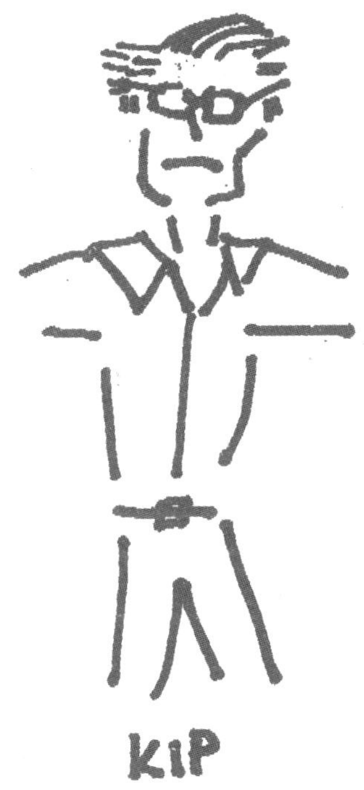

Ike Ferguson

One afternoon when Roy was riding with his uncle, Buck Colby, in Buck's Cadillac, Roy, who was thirteen years old, saw an old man hobbling along a path next to the road, balancing himself with a cane in each hand. Despite the extremely warm, humid weather, the old man was wearing a tweed jacket and a large burlap cap. Roy's uncle noticed him, too, pulled the car to the side of the road several yards ahead of the aged pedestrian, and stopped.

"Why are you stopping, Unk? For the old man?"

"Yes, Roy. I know him. His name is Ike Ferguson. He lives near here with his grandson's family. He must be almost ninety years old now."

"How do you know him?"

"I sold a house to his son, Moses, back in Chicago. Ike lived with him until Moses died about twenty years ago. Ike was taken in by Moses's oldest son, Nathan, and came to live with him and his family here in Tampa."

Buck got out of the car, so Roy did, too. They stood by the rear fender and waited for Ike Ferguson to get there.

"Hello, Ike," said Buck. "You're looking spry as ever, galli-vanting up the road."

The old man halted and looked at Buck. He was clean-shaven, not wearing spectacles or hearing aids, and had on a clean white shirt and black tie underneath the coat.

"Hello there, Colby. Wie geht's?"

"Fine. Where are you headed? Can my nephew and I give you a lift? He's visiting from Chicago."

"Nein. I'm getting my exercise. It's difficult enough without having to get around your big car."

"I'll move it."

"Danke schöen. I have to keep up. To stop is to die."

"Let's go, Roy. Good to see you, Ike."

Buck and Roy got back into the car and Buck drove away. Roy looked out the rear window and watched the old man plodding ahead.

"How come he spoke some words in German, Unk?"

"How do you know he was speaking German, Roy?"

"John, the janitor at our building, is from Germany. He taught me a few words. Is Ike Ferguson from Germany, too?"

"He was, forty or fifty years ago. He was speaking Yiddish, a kind of gutter German."

"Ferguson is an Irish name. I have a friend named Jimmy Ferguson. His family is from Ireland."

"Ike was an immigrant before the war, Roy. When he came through Ellis Island in New York, a Customs officer asked him in English what his name was. Ike didn't know English and he didn't have any identification papers. The Customs officer kept asking him but Ike didn't answer. Finally he said, 'Ich vergessen,' I've forgotten. So the Customs man said, 'Okay, you're Ike Ferguson now.' Then he stamped an entry permit, handed it to Ike, and allowed him to pass into the United States. After all these years he still has a strong Yiddish accent. He's Jewish, not Irish, he made his living as a carpenter. I hired him once to build a staircase. In Chicago, he lived in an Irish neighborhood and because he had an Irish name and was so likeable the community came to consider him an honorary Irishman. He even became a member of the local Tipperary Club, which was exclusively for men of Irish descent."

"Jimmy Ferguson and his parents are Catholics. Did Ike become a Catholic, too?"

"No, Roy, he didn't go that far."

"For such an old man, he's in pretty good shape."

"He's got all his marbles, too. Ike was always a great reader, and he has a sharp sense of humor. I remember a joke he told me. A girl from a very poor family in Donegal left Ireland dressed practically in rags and returned to her village a year or more later wearing good clothes, looking quite prosperous. She encountered an old priest on the street she'd known since childhood who commented on her fine appearance and asked her where she'd been and what she'd been doing there.

"'I've been in London, Father,' she said. 'I've become a prostitute.'

"'What?!' he said, visibly alarmed.

"'A prostitute, Father,' she repeated.

"'Oh,' said the priest, clearly relieved. 'I thought you said you'd become a Protestant.'"

Navigating the Unexpected

When Roy was eighteen years old and traveling through Europe, he went into the Traveler's Aid office in the railroad station at Ghent, Belgium, to find out how to get to Zeveneken, a nearby town where a friend of his lived. A man in the office who'd come to check a train schedule told Roy he'd show him where to catch the bus and led him outside to the front of the station. He spoke English and showed Roy on the post at the stop that the next bus for Zeveneken was not due to leave for almost four hours. He said that his wife and child were due in at about the same time on a train from Antwerp. He looked Roy over carefully and asked if he was hungry. Roy told him he was.

"Come on then," he said. "You can come home with me for a while and we will eat. Then I will drive you back here."

Roy was very hungry and decided to go along. The man was small, in his forties, pasty-faced but with very dark eyes and hair. He spoke English with a strange accent, definitely not French or Flemish.

"You're not from Belgium originally, are you?" Roy asked him.

They were in the man's *deux chevaux*, trundling down a cobblestone street. Ghent looked to Roy like a storybook land. Even the rain had stopped, leaving everything glistening, immaculate. He was glad to be out of Paris.

"I am Russian, from Minsk. My name is Bulgakov."

"Did you learn English in Russia? You speak perfectly."

"I lived in the United States for fourteen years. I was a navigator on boats, first in the Gulf of Mexico, then on the Great Lakes. I lived for two years in Galveston, Texas, then for twelve years outside Chicago."

"I grew up mostly in Chicago," Roy told Bulgakov. "Where did you live there?"

"In Lincolnwood," he said. "On Laramie Street."

Roy laughed. "Really? My Uncle Buck lived for several years on Laramie Street in Lincolnwood. He was in the construction business and built most of the houses in that part of town."

Bulgakov looked at Roy and half smiled. "Colby Construction Company, yes? Your uncle was Buck Colby?"

"Yes! Were you a neighbor of his? I used to spend a lot of time there."

"My father and I bought a house from your uncle. He was a good fellow, it was a good house."

"That's amazing," said Roy. "Does your father still live there?"

"No, he is dead."

Bulgakov

"What a coincidence, though, your knowing my Uncle Buck."

Roy introduced himself and they shook hands as the man drove.

"Why did you come here?" Roy asked. "Are you still a navigator?"

"No, I don't work on boats now. I am a stateless person, allowed to remain because my wife and son are Belgian citizens. My wife works and I take care of the boy and the house. Also, I am writing a book about what happened to me in America."

Roy was about to ask what had happened to him in America when Bulgakov pulled the car into the driveway of a modest but handsome two-story house on a short street.

"This is a nice place," Roy said as they got out of the car.

Bulgakov again gave him a half smile. "We'll go in," he said. "I'll make you some dinner and I will tell you a story about your country."

As Roy ate the wonderful meal Bulgakov prepared—steak, spinach, potatoes, salad, bread, cake—he told Roy how during the fifties, because he was Russian, he had been blacklisted as a Communist and prevented from working on ships in the United States.

"I was *not* a Communist. It was because of Stalin that my father and I left the Soviet Union and went to America. My mother and sister were murdered by the pig Stalin. America was *freedom*! We were good citizens. My father could not speak English, only a little. He was too old to learn, but I became a citizen, I studied hard, and then the government says I am a spy and I cannot work."

"Did they prosecute you? As a spy, I mean."

"No. They *per*secuted me, made sure I could not get a job on a seagoing vessel anywhere in the country. The unions would do nothing for me, pretended I was dead. So much for the so-called 'commie' unions! Wait, I'll show you something."

Bulgakov went upstairs and returned a few minutes later, carrying a large box.

"These are the letters," Bulgakov said, pulling papers from the box. "Letters and documents from the ten years I spent clearing my name. I spent ten thousand dollars in legal fees to prove that I was not a Communist, to make the government allow me to work again on boats, to remove my name from the blacklist. It took all those years and all that money to accomplish this. My father died, not only from old age but shame and pain, knowing the accusations were false. We had to sell the house your uncle built so that we could have money to live. Nobody would hire me. I was a 'security risk.' Such shit it was. Finally I did it, I cleared my name, and when I did I left America and came here, first to Brussels, where I knew some people, then, after I married, to Ghent. I gave up my American passport, renounced my citizenship that I had studied so hard to earn. I am a free citizen now. I live here, I hope I will die here. Do you want more coffee?"

"No, no thank you. I can't eat any more. That's a terrible story."

"Yes, terrible, but there are many worse stories, of course. Especially in the Soviet Union. That is the only place worse than the United States."

They drove back to the train station, where Bulgakov met his wife, a pretty red-haired woman, and their two-year-old son. He told his wife that Roy was a "stray" from America, that he'd given him a meal and allowed him to freshen up at their house. Roy felt better not only for having eaten but Bulgakov had also insisted that he take a bath and shave. Roy was extremely grateful for the hospitality he told Bulgakov's wife, and would be glad to return the same if ever they came to America.

"Thank you but no," said Bulgakov, not smiling as he spoke. "My wife and son don't need that other kind of hospitality I was so privileged to receive, the kind that is beyond your control."

He took his wife and son to the car and then walked Roy to the bus stop.

"So, good-bye, my friend," Bulgakov said, shaking Roy's hand. "Please do not thank me anymore. I want you to know I loved the United States, I loved the house your uncle built, it was a fine house. I am sorry but I will never see it again. I don't *have* to stay here. I *want* to. I am a free man. Good-bye."

Bulgakov walked back to his car. The bus to Zeveneken arrived and Roy got on. He took a window seat and looked back. Bulgakov was holding up his son and talking to him.

When Roy told his uncle about meeting Bulgakov, Buck remembered him and recalled that he'd actually sold the house to the elder Bulgakov. Buck knew that the son had had some difficulty with the government, but he hadn't known the extent of Bulgakov's problem and didn't know why he'd sold the house.

"Pretty strange, my meeting Bulgakov like that in Ghent, don't you think?"

"Well, Roy, the older I get, the more I believe that there's no such thing as a bad coincidence."

Roy at 18

The Law of Affection

Roy's Uncle Buck had big plans for his investment in Honduras. In the early 1970s, he bought a piece of property on the island of Utila, in the Bay Islands, off the coast across from La Ceiba. He owned fifteen hundred feet of beachfront and envisioned a vacation paradise that included gambling—which was legal in Honduras—luxury hotels, sailing, speedboats, etc. Buck, who was a civil engineer, built himself an octagonal house on stilts; when the tide came in it was necessary to use a boat to get to dry land. For this purpose, he kept a dinghy with a small outboard motor tied to one of the stilts next to a ladder. A person could easily swim to shore, he told Roy, but the bay was shark-infested, which rendered that option a bit risky.

Buck claimed the island was governed by witchcraft, or voodoo, but in reality the few hundred inhabitants, who were mostly descendants of pirates, slave traders and slaves, and who bore surnames such as Morgan, Jones, and Lafitte, were motivated and inspired more by superstition than anything else. The people were very poor, and, Roy's uncle's grandiose ideas notwithstanding, there was virtually no tourism during the twenty years he lived there.

There was, however, soon after Buck sold his property on Utila, a terrible hurricane that devastated much of the Bay Islands, as well as Tegucigalpa, the capital of the country. Roy's uncle had a good life there for a while. He was about sixty when he moved to Utila,

REPUBLICA DE HONDURAS

and he soon acquired Juana, who was then sixteen, as his island girl. Buck spoke fluent Spanish and taught Juana English. She took care of the property when he was away, and, years later, when Juana wanted to immigrate to the United States, Buck helped her gain residency in Tampa, Florida, where he also kept a home. Juana eventually married a man in Tampa and she and Buck remained good friends until the end of his life. In fact, she was at his bedside in the hospital when he died, two weeks before what would have been his ninety-third birthday.

When Roy was twelve, visiting his uncle in Tampa, Buck told him that Bobby Robinson, a friend of his on the island, had been arrested for shooting to death a mutual acquaintance of theirs named George Morgan. Robinson and Morgan had been at a picnic with their families and friends when a dispute arose over a card game. Apparently the two men, who were both in their late twenties, and who had known each other all of their lives, had argued heatedly for a short time, then stopped. The others present thought it was finished, but an hour or so later Bobby, who may have been drunk, took a pistol and fired a bullet into George Morgan's left temple, killing him instantly.

Buck received a letter a couple of weeks after this incident occurred from another friend on the island, Spurgeon Bush, who owned the only appliance store there. Bush, who had been at the picnic, told Buck what happened and that Bobby Robinson was being held in the island jail. Roy's uncle placed a call to his friend Prince Albert, the sheriff, at the jail, and Bobby Robinson answered the telephone.

"Bobby, what are you doing answering the phone?" asked Buck. "I thought you were being held on a murder charge."

"I'm playing checkers with Prince Albert," Bobby said, "at his desk, so when it rang I just picked it up."

"Did you shoot Morgan?"

"Yes," said Bobby, "but it was an accident. Prince Albert says he's going to release me as soon as the investigation has been completed."

"Let me talk to Albert. Buena suerte, Bobby."

"Gracias, Señor Buck. Hasta pronto."

Bobby passed the receiver to Prince Albert and Buck asked him for the details.

"Bobby didn't mean to shoot George Morgan," the sheriff told him. "And nobody minds that Morgan is dead. He was an unpopular fellow, as you know."

"Were there any witnesses?"

"Very many witnesses," said Prince Albert. "I have collected many statements already. Everyone says Bobby did not mean to kill Morgan. It was an old gun with a faulty firing pin. Bobby didn't think it would go off."

"But it did," said Buck.

"For better or worse, yes," replied the sheriff.

"What about Morgan's family? He had a wife and a child, didn't he? Who's going to take care of them?"

"Morgan's wife, Victoria, is Bobby's first cousin," said Prince Albert. "He says she will be all right with his family. Victoria was not happy with Morgan. She will find another man. Maybe me. Victoria is very pretty still, you remember."

"I don't think I know her."

"You will. When you return to the island, we will invite you to my house for supper."

A couple of years later, in his uncle's house, Roy met Spurgeon Bush, the appliance store proprietor. They were sitting in the guest bedroom. Spurgeon always called Roy sobrino, nephew in Spanish. He showed Roy a silver-plated .38 he said he always carried and a business card on which was printed a telephone number and the name of a general in the Honduran army.

"Turn over the card," Spurgeon said. "Read the words written above the signature."

"Este hombre esta bajo mi proteccion."

"These are the six most important words to possess in my country. This is my permiso."

"Your permission for what?" Roy asked him.

"To kill," said Spurgeon. "I am a special agent under the authority of the general. Nobody will harm me."

"What about the appliance business?"

"What about it?"

"If I angered you by buying a refrigerator from another store, you could shoot me and not be charged with murder."

Spurgeon Bush smiled, revealing several gold teeth. "You forget, sobrino, I am the only refrigerator dealer on Utila."

Roy handed him back his permiso.

"Unlike others in Honduras," Spurgeon said, "I use my gun only for the most high reasons."

"What about Bobby Robinson? Did he have a good reason to shoot George Morgan?"

"The best. Victoria, Morgan's wife, was Bobby's first cousin, but they had been lovers since they were children. The child was Bobby's, not Morgan's."

"Morgan knew this?"

Spurgeon shrugged his shoulders.

"Did Bobby have a permiso, also?"

"No, otherwise Prince Albert would not have been able to arrest him. But Bobby had the right."

"I would think, as Victoria's husband," Roy said, "that George Morgan, if he knew the child was not his, would have had the right to kill Bobby."

Spurgeon stood up and tucked the silver-plated .38 into his waistband. He was wearing powder-blue beltless slacks and a jungle-green guayabera. Spurgeon was not particularly tall but he was stocky with hands like meat cleavers. His skin was what they called on the island pardo, mud brown, and his face was riddled with pock marks. He had a deep scar on his nose shaped like an anchor.

Spurgeon Bush smiled at Roy again and laid a meat cleaver on one of his shoulders.

"*Sobrino*," he said, "nobody liked George Morgan."

Shock Treatment

"Did you ever get mixed up with a woman who wanted you to kill her husband so that she could be with you?"

"No, why?"

"It happened to me."

"Did you do it?"

"Of course not. I told her to leave me alone or I might kill her."

"Then what?"

"I heard she got someone to do it."

"Who is she?"

"This was years ago, in New York. I don't know where she lives now."

"Were you in love with her?"

"Not enough to knock off her husband. You can't ever really know how crazy anyone is. It scares me. I'll see you later, Buck."

"Poker night. Seven o'clock, right?"

Gus nodded and left Buck's office. Buck thought about what Gus had just told him. It reminded him of a woman he'd gone around with for a little while before he moved to Tampa. Diana Antonelli. She'd murdered a boy when she was sixteen, an eighteen-year-old college kid she was dating. Diana had told Buck about it, that the boy had gotten her pregnant, refused to marry her, and denied he was the father. She'd become hysterical and stabbed him to death with a kitchen knife at her family's house. Shortly thereafter she'd had a miscarriage, was declared temporarily insane in juvenile court, then was packed off by her parents to a private residence operated by a psychiatric clinic in Kansas where she was kept—imprisoned, Diana said—for almost two years.

All of that had transpired fifteen years before Buck met her. At the time, Diana was living alone and working as a clerical assistant in an attorney's office. She was smart, pretty, and fun to be with. Neither she nor Buck had been married, they got along well; their relationship, while affectionate, Buck did not consider serious. When one night Diana related to him her history, she did so calmly, and said that the Diana who had committed the murder was a sister who no longer existed. Confused, Buck asked her what happened to her sister. Diana said she didn't know, only that it was as if she had never really lived. Buck then asked Diana if she had undergone shock treatments at the clinic in Kansas. Again she said she didn't know, that her sister had never told her if she had.

Buck saw Diana only a couple of times after hearing her story, and after he left Chicago they did not stay in touch. Gus's experience with the woman in New York had not been the same as his with Diana Antonelli, but like Gus he knew he would always wonder what happened to her.

Anna Louise

Roy's cousin Skip's mother, Anna Louise, was an alcoholic. The first thing she did every morning after she got out of bed was go into the kitchen and put a teaspoon of sugar into a chimney-sized glass, fill it with gin, stir it up, and drink half of it. Then she lit a gold-papered, unfiltered cigarette and took a long drag before finishing off her glass of gin. She was a natural platinum blonde with unblemished ghost-white skin. Anna Louise was Roy's Uncle Buck's first wife; after him, she married Karl von Sydow, a Swedish construction magnate. Von Sydow died of a heart attack six years after marrying Anna Louise and left his fortune to her. She and Skip, who was fifteen when von Sydow died, lived north of Chicago on an estate fronted by a high brick wall. A stream ran through thick woods that bordered the other three sides of the property. Anna Louise owned the land the woods and stream were on. She was forty-two and still beautiful when her second husband died. After she'd drunk the glassful of gin, she puffed on her cigarette for a minute or two before returning to the bathroom that adjoined the master bedroom and began running water into the sunken tub. She remained entirely nude during this routine no matter who else was in the house. Roy was thirteen when he first witnessed his aunt's diurnal performance. Anna Louise had perfect posture, having as a girl and young woman been a dancer and an actress before working briefly as a teacher of calculus and poetry at a private girls' school. She was twenty-two when she married

Roy's uncle, who, Anna Louise unembarrassedly informed Roy, had not been her first lover, though she had let him believe so.

"Your uncle was good to me and an ardent paramour," she said, "until he impregnated me. After that, I seldom saw him. It wasn't much of a marriage. Von Sydow was consistently hands-on, shall I say. I don't know which was worse. I should have married a Jew."

Roy's aunt delivered this information to him while he and his cousin Skip were seated at the breakfast table eating cereal, the only food Anna Louise kept in the house. She had yet to run her bath.

Roy saw her infrequently during his teenage years, the last time being when he was seventeen and she was living in a motel in an unfashionable suburb of the city. This was after she had unintentionally set fire to her house, which burned to the ground. Anna Louise had passed out drunk in her bedroom, where firemen found her collapsed on the floor and carried her out just before the roof caved in.

According to Skip, most of his mother's money was gone, swindled by von Sydow's attorney, whom she had trusted to manage her financial affairs, and she spent the majority of her waking hours drinking gin out of the bottle from a case on the floor next to her bed positioned so that to extract a new bottle all she had to do was reach down and lift it up to her lips.

The last Roy heard of Anna Louise was that she had been admitted to an assisted living facility in Indiana, where she had relatives. By that time, however, her mind was gone, as well as what little money she had left, and she died sober and fully dressed sitting in a wheelchair. Skip was overseas in the army at the time and did not come back for the funeral, which was paid for by his father.

Roy always remembered Anna Louise naked in the morning in her big house standing in the kitchen holding her tall glass of sugared gin and a golden cigarette; but he never understood what she meant when she said she should have married a Jew.

The Sun and Other Stars

"'Be kind to me.' It's a line that's been used in more than a hundred movies. I've heard it several times myself, and after the first time it's always made me laugh."

"Not the first time?"

"No, I fell for it. She was a good actress. It took almost four years before I realized it was a throwaway, a weapon in every vamp's playbook."

"Why so long?"

"I was young. After I figured it out I was disappointed, of course."

"Did it make you sad?"

"A little, but not unhappy. I was still alive and ready for the next time."

Parris Island

"I spent the summer I was sixteen on Parris Island, South Carolina, where my brother, Buck, was stationed with the navy. Our mother was married then to her second husband and they didn't want me around. I left boarding school and two days later I was put on a train at Union Station in Chicago. Buck was married to his first wife, Katarina, and since he was already a commissioned officer—a lieutenant commander—they had a nice apartment off the base.

"Katarina was a party giver, she liked to entertain, to have company. They even had a grand piano in the living room, which she encouraged me to play during their cocktail gatherings. Popular songs, 'Stardust,' 'You Stepped Out of a Dream,' 'Stars Fell on Alabama.' I was pretty good, I'd taken lessons since I was five, and my mother could play and sing. Most of the guests were officers and their wives, many of whom complimented me, and after they'd had a couple of Buck's martinis one or more of the men made suggestive remarks to me. Katarina protected me, though. She was very smart, she'd taught calculus and read poetry by Ezra Pound and T.S. Eliot. She was lousy elegant, sophisticated but unpretentious, she kept control of the scene. I liked her and admired her looks. She was a natural platinum blonde, a bit severe looking but attractive. She wore her hair pulled back tightly against her skull, which exaggerated her high ckeekbones and wide mouth. My brother was at his handsomest, he resembled Errol Flynn or Ronald Colman. The wives of the other officers were crazy for him. To her credit,

Katarina got a kick out of their sometimes shameless behavior. She made sure these women knew he was her property and she revelled in their envy. I was quite shy at that time. I was impressed by Katarina's casually icy savoir-faire. Being in that atmosphere was a treat for me after having spent several months at Our Lady of Everlasting Obedience. I had a good time that summer on Parris Island."

"My, Kitty," said Polly Page, "it's fun to hear you talk about yourself. Are you this forthcoming when you see your psychiatrist?"

"Oh, no. I only saw him a couple of times. He prescribed pills that made me dopey. June DeLisa sent me to him, she lives on those pills. There was no way I could open up to him. I can't talk to men, I never could."

"Even your husbands?"

"Especially them. I tell stories about my life to Roy, he's a good listener."

"He's only eight years old, Kitty. He's incapable of understanding your innermost feelings about things, you can't share your most intimate thoughts."

Kitty lit a cigarette and looked out the dining-room window. Daylight was disappearing.

"Buck went to prison for two years. Did you know that?"

"No. What for?"

"While he was in the navy, as a civil engineer he was in charge of handing out construction contracts to private companies. He took bribes and got caught. I was eighteen. My father visited him when he was in the military penitentiary in New Hampshire."

"What happed to Katarina?"

"She divorced him after he got out. I remember when he was living in a one-room basement apartment with a bare bulb hanging from the ceiling on LaSalle Street. It really made me sad."

"Did you ever talk to him about any of this?"

"I only asked him one question: 'What happened to the grand piano?' "

Both women laughed, and Polly said, "Katarina took it."

"Of course. Buck said she sold it for much less than it was worth."

After Polly left, Kitty recalled the time she was six years old, walking on a sidewalk with Buck, who had just graduated from the University of Alabama and was back in Chicago for a brief visit, when a loose, snarling, barking dog approached them. Buck moved in front of Kitty, as he did so shielding her behind him. He spoke calmly to the dog and it slowly backed off, though continuing to growl and bare its big yellow teeth. Buck and Kitty passed by without altering their pace and the dog kept its distance. Kitty asked Buck what he'd said to prevent it from attacking them and he told her, "It wasn't what I said, it was how I said it."

The light had gone but Kitty did not turn on a lamp. If the phone rang she wouldn't answer it.

THE
PRESIDENT
OF
THE UNITED STATES OF AMERICA

To all who shall see these presents, greeting:

Know Ye, that reposing special trust and confidence in the patriotism, valor, fidelity and abilities of Buck [redacted] Colby I do appoint him First Lieutenant in the Corps of Engineers in

The Army of the United States

such appointment to date from the twenty-second day of September nineteen hundred and thirty-six. He is therefore carefully and diligently to discharge the duty of the office to which he is appointed by doing and performing all manner of things thereunto belonging.

He will enter upon active duty under this commission only when specifically ordered to such active duty by competent authority.

And I do strictly charge and require all Officers and Soldiers under his command when he shall be employed on active duty to be obedient to his orders as an officer of his grade and position. And he is to observe and follow such orders and directions from time to time as he shall receive from me, or the future President of the United States of America, or the General or other Superior Officers set over him, according to the rules and discipline of War.

This Commission evidences an appointment in the Army of the United States under the provisions of section 37, National Defense Act, as amended, and is to continue in force for a period of five years from the date above specified, and during the pleasure of the President of the United States for the time being.

Done at the City of Washington, this thirteenth day of November in the year of our Lord one thousand nine hundred and thirty-six and of the Independence of the United States of America the one hundred and sixty-first

By the President:

Adjutant General.

The Grasshopper

"We love you baby girl! Keep it up kiddo! I'll be waiting for you tonight! XOXO, Cahyani"

Walking back from the river Roy found this note written on a piece of white paper cut into the shape of a heart on the sidewalk. He saw the piece of paper with writing on it, picked it up, read it, and put it into a pocket of his jacket. He figured the person to whom it was given or sent had dropped it accidentally.

Roy was staying with his Uncle Buck while his mother was away on a trip with her boyfriend, Pablo Puñetazo, to his home country of Venezuela. Roy was nine years old. When he got to his uncle's house he asked Buck what kind of name Cahyani was.

Buck was just finishing mixing himself a grasshopper. He took a sip, then said, "Cahyani? I'm not sure. Hawaiian, maybe, Polynesian. Why?"

"I found a note on the street. Take a look."

Roy handed it to his uncle.

"I've never seen or heard this name before. Probably a girl lost it on her way to or from school. There aren't many Pacific Islanders here in Tampa."

Buck gave the note back to Roy.

"I knew a girl in Washington, DC, when I was in the navy named Leilani, just after the war. She was engaged to marry an admiral. I was a lieutenant commander then. We met at a cocktail party for officers. Leilani told me she'd dated the admiral, who was much older than she, when he was stationed in Honolulu, where she was from. Leilani knew how to talk to men, she liked me, so I saw her a few times while I was in DC. She told me the admiral thought she was out shopping in the afternoons."

"Did the admiral ever find out that you were fooling around with her?"

"I don't know about ever, but not when she and I were meeting. At least I don't think so. Leilani hadn't had much formal education, she wasn't book smart, but she was savvy. She told me she'd started working as a hostess in a bar when she was sixteen."

"Does that mean she was a prostitute?"

Buck took another sip of his grasshopper.

"A little too sweet," he said. "Too much crème de cacao."

"What's in that drink, Unk? How come it's green?"

"Crème de menthe, which gives it a greenish tint; white crème de cacao, which tastes like chocolate; heavy cream and ice; with a little nutmeg sprinkled on top. I rarely get the balance just right."

"Was Leilani beautiful?"

"I guess so. Her skin was sort of the color of this grasshopper, only darker. No, Roy, she wasn't a prostitute. Leilani was a poor girl who used her looks to get what she needed. There's nothing wrong with that."

Buck held out his glass toward Roy.

"Here, nephew, have a sip. Pretend it's what Leilani tasted like."

Leilani

Shrimpers

Roy and his friend Willy Duda were looking for a summer job. They were both fourteen years old and temporary work that paid decently in Tampa, Florida, in 1961, was hard to find. Tampa was a small southern city then, a fishing and cigar town with a large ethnic Cuban population. Roy's Uncle Buck, with whom Roy lived during the summer months, was in the construction business; he would have employed both his nephew and Willy Duda, as he had in better times, but the building trade was slow at the moment so the boys had to look elsewhere to make money. Buck, who had been a lieutenant commander in the navy during the Second World War, suggested they sign up to work on a shrimp boat.

"These little boats have small crews," Buck told them, "usually only the captain and two or three helpers. The boats go out for ten days, two weeks, maybe three at most, then bring in their catch, sell it, take a few days off, and go back out again. Come on, I'll take you down to the docks and we'll see if someone needs hands."

Roy and Willy didn't know anything about shrimping but Roy's uncle said the work was pretty simple. It was a cloudless, sunny day, as usual, and Buck talked while he drove.

"You toss out the nets into the shrimp beds, haul 'em in and load 'em in a cooler. It's repetitious, hard work, and there's nothing to do but work on a shrimp boat in the middle of the Gulf of Mexico. You sleep on deck."

"It's hot as Hades out there," said Willy. "We'll fry like catfish being on the water twenty-four hours a day."

"You boys can hold up for a fortnight," Buck said. "It'll be a good experience."

The shrimp boats docked under the Simon Bolívar Bridge. Roy's uncle drove his 1957 Cadillac Eldorado convertible right onto the wharf, parked, and he and the two boys got out. Most of the boats were empty or their captains were asleep under a canopy. Buck, Willy, and Roy walked along the wooden planks until they came upon a man in a boat mending nets. The boat's name, painted on the stern in faded black letters, was *Lazarus*.

"Ahoy there, captain," Roy's uncle called out to him. "I've got a couple of strong young men here looking for work. Are you hiring?"

The man had a lobster-red face with a six-day beard and a dead cigar sticking out of the right side of his mouth. Roy thought he looked to be about forty years old, maybe older. The man's left eye was closed and did not open during the time he spoke to them. He was wearing a sleeveless green sweatshirt inside out that had brown and black stains on it.

"These boys are young but they're able-bodied," Buck shouted.

The man took a quick look up at Roy and Willy then returned his attention to the nets.

"Too young," he said. "A shrimp boat ain't no place for clean-cut kids. Only lowlifes work shrimpers. Alkys, criminals, cutthroats, perverts. Nothin' to do but haul, mend, swill bad hooch like the devil's slaves, and bugger each other."

"Maybe this isn't such a good idea, Unk," said Roy.

Two weeks later he and Willy were watching the TV news when a picture of the shrimp boat captain Buck had talked to came on the screen followed by a female reporter standing on the dock under the Bolívar Bridge.

"Albert Matanzas," said the reporter, "captain and owner of a shrimp boat out of Tampa, was discovered by the Coast Guard drifting in Tampa Bay close to death tied with a rope to the wheel of his boat with stab wounds in his left arm and shoulder and a bullet wound in his right leg. Two men were lying dead from gunshots on the deck. According to a statement Captain Matanzas gave to the Coast Guard, a third man was lost overboard in the Gulf after being shot by one of the dead men. It has not yet been determined what caused the dispute among the men. Matanzas remains in critical condition in Tampa General Hospital."

"Let's not ask your uncle if he has any more ideas," said Willy.

Streator

"You ever run into a guy named Bill Small, sometimes called Shorty? From a town near Chicago, your old neck of the woods."

Buck shook his head. "What's his game?"

"Button man, independent. Only arrested once, far as we know. Got off, insufficient evidence. That was in Chi, three years ago."

"Who'd he kill?"

"A federal judge Mosca couldn't put in his pocket."

"So?"

Gus Argo shrugged. "Forty-six years in the rackets and Mosca's never spent a night in jail, let alone been convicted of a crime."

"Why are you asking me? I've been in Tampa since nineteen fifty-nine, almost seven years."

"You meet all kinds of people, Buck. You know Traficante."

Buck laughed. "I'm in the construction business, Gus. Tampa's not Chicago."

"Getting bigger."

"I met Santo in Havana, in the old days. We both live here, sometimes I run into him in the Columbia restaurant. He owns a piece of it."

"Like almost every other place in Ybor City. He's not an easy man to get in to see."

"Try the Columbia, the ropa vieja there is excellent."

Gus Argo stood up. "We've been friends for a long time, Buck, since the war. I hope we're still on the same side."

Buck stood up and walked around his desk. The two men shook hands.

"Why shouldn't we be? You don't have to remind me how old I am."

After Argo left the office, Buck looked at a framed photograph of himself in his lieutenant commander's uniform on the wall behind the desk. He and Gus Argo had both been in the OSS before the war, then in the Seabees in the South Pacific. When Gus joined the FBI he contacted Buck and asked him if he was interested in coming along, an offer Buck declined. He never wanted to belong to any organization again; as a civil engineer he went into the building trades, a decision he did not regret. Buck knew that should he encounter or learn the whereabouts of Bill Small he would find a way to anonymously pass the information on to Gus Argo.

A couple of months later Buck read an item in the *Tampa Tribune* saying the body of a man found floating under a pier in Tampa Bay had been identified from information found on the corpse as that of William Small, a resident of Streator, Illinois. According to harbor police, Small had not been reported as a missing person. Anyone wishing to claim the body was instructed to do so at the city morgue within the next seven days, after which the body would be interred in the Hillsborough County cemetery for the indigent.

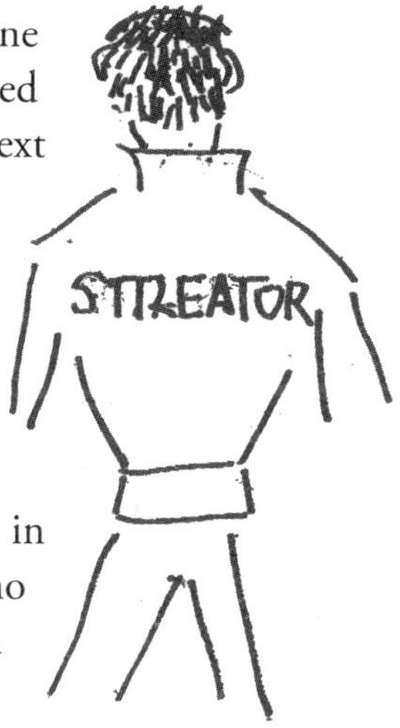

Buck clipped the item from the newspaper and mailed it to Gus Argo at his office in Washington, DC. He remembered an older kid he'd known in high school in Chicago named Billy who had been an amateur boxing champion in his former home town of Streator, Illinois.

Billy always wore a gray athletic jacket with STREATOR printed across the back and a red-and-white badge on the chest with the words Lightweight Champion Streator A.A.U. 1928 on it above a pair of boxing gloves. He was a short guy.

Yukon Story

Roy's Uncle Buck, his mother's brother, who was fourteen years older than Kitty, had been working in Alaska building a railroad through the Yukon Territory when he got pleurisy and came to stay with his sister, mother, and Roy at their apartment in Chicago while he recuperated. Buck was forty years old then, a civil and mechanical engineer. He'd been in the Yukon for three months through the late fall and early winter of 1952. Roy was seven and enjoyed listening to his uncle's stories about clearing forests and laying down tracks, hearing moose calls and wolf howls during the long frigid nights, and the occasional fights among the laborers that sometimes involved gun battles.

"Were any of the men killed?" Roy asked him.

"Only one that I know of, nephew. Almost everybody up there carries a gun or a knife."

"Did you?"

"Yes, a .357. It's in my duffel bag."

"I don't want a gun in my house," said Rose, Roy's grandmother.

"Don't worry, Ma," Buck said, "it's locked in a case and unloaded."

They were all in the kitchen. Roy's mother was frying eggs and bacon on the stove for breakfast.

"Put on a shirt, son," Rose told Buck, "it's freezing cold in here."

Buck was wearing only pajama bottoms and his feet were bare.

He laughed and said, "Cold? This isn't cold. It was thirty below in the Yukon."

Buck picked up a strip of bacon from a wrapper on the counter, held it in front of his face, and took a bite.

"Buck!" Kitty shouted. "You can't eat raw bacon! You'll get sick."

"All the boys up north eat it right out of the package."

Buck nibbled the bacon until he'd devoured the entire strip.

"Your uncle's crazy, Roy," said Kitty. "Don't do what he does."

"Did you see any wolves, Unk?"

"A few, but they mostly kept their distance from our camp. Noise from the trucks, skinners, and bulldozers frightened them away."

"Are you going back after you feel better?"

"I don't think so, Roy. It's already the middle of January and the job is scheduled to wrap up in March."

Buck was divorced; his eleven–year-old son, Kip, had been sent by his mother, Katarina, to live with her father, Doc Wurtzel, in Mexico until she was resettled. Katarina was an alcoholic, so Buck thought it was better for Kip to live for now at Doc's hacienda in Cuernavaca.

"Are you going to live in Chicago?"

"I'm going to open an office downtown, nephew, and start my own engineering firm. I want to work for myself from now on."

"Come on," said Kitty, "let's all sit down and eat. The coffee's ready, Buck."

"One of our sled dogs bit a thermos in half one morning and scalded himself so bad that he was blinded and had to be shot. Big husky named Bulletproof. The ground was frozen so hard he couldn't be buried, so the Eskimo boys skinned and ate him."

"Did you eat dog, Unk? How did it taste?"

"Buck will tell you later, Roy," said his grandmother. "Finish your eggs."

Years later, after his mother, grandmother, and Buck were dead, Roy found the steel-toed boots his uncle had worn when he was in the Yukon in a steamer trunk in the garage of Kitty's house. The leather was stiff, of course, but Roy tried them on anyway. They were too small for Roy, which surprised him because he always thought of Buck as being bigger than he was. Nothing else in the trunk could Roy identify as having belonged to his uncle. The boots had probably been packed away in there since the winter of '52.

Roy remembered his uncle telling him that one of the work crew in the Yukon, a man named Morrison, told Buck that when he was nineteen years old, laying track in Nome, he'd gotten frostbite so extreme that he'd had to have all of the toes on his left foot amputated. Morrison learned how to walk by putting most of his weight on his right foot, balancing on the toes. The bones in the small toes of that foot kept breaking, though, so when he was twenty-six, he cut them off himself with a hacksaw. He left the big toe attached. Buck asked Morrison how long ago he'd lopped off four of the toes on his right foot and Morrison said, "Must be eight since I'm thirty-four now." He went on to tell Buck that getting rid of those toes had improved his balance. He always stuffed a heavy sock inside the front of his boots. Buck asked Morrison why he hadn't cut off the big toe, too. "Just in case," said Morrison. "In case of what?" asked Buck. Morrison laughed and said, "You never know when another toe could come in handy."

Los Apuros

When Roy was fifteen his Uncle Buck, who lived in Tampa, Florida, asked Roy to help him crew a sailboat from Nassau, in the Bahamas, across the ocean to Coral Gables. Buck also invited a friend of his named Manuel Montiel from Honduras, where Buck owned a house on the Bay island of Utila. Roy and his uncle drove from Tampa to Miami, from where they flew to Nassau. Manuel joined them there and together they met the owner of the boat, Nate Truman, with whom Buck had become acquainted during a gambling junket to Paradise Island.

Nate had invited Buck, whom he learned was an experienced sailor, to sail the *Varmint* first to Bimini, then to Florida for renovation of the galley and some minor repairs. He assured Buck that the *Varmint* was seaworthy, a thirty-seven-foot Morgan, and offered to pay all expenses. Truman was in his late sixties, a retired businessman from Ohio, where he had once been the mayor of a small town. Manuel Montiel was a short, slender thirty-year-old man who introduced himself to Roy as *un tipo de la hampa*, which Buck translated as "a guy from the underworld," without further explanation.

Everything went according to plan until they got caught in a storm within sight of the lights of Miami. It was four o'clock in the morning, raining hard. Buck was standing lookout on the bow, Roy was at the tiller, Manuel was tending to the sails, and Nate Truman was below deck stowing away unsecured gear. Sud-

denly Manuel began shouting, "Peligro por delante! Peligro por delante! Darse vuelta!"

Roy stood up, keeping one hand on the tiller, and saw a tree ahead close to the bow. He sat down and with both of his feet pushed the tiller away from him as hard as he could and held it there until and as the *Varmint* began to come about. As quickly as he could, Manuel adjusted the sails and within thirty seconds the boat veered to port and came about no more than three feet from a tiny islet.

Nate came on deck, saw where they were, and said to Roy, "Why didn't Buck warn you? Didn't he see that island?"

"I guess not," said Roy.

"Buck!" Nate shouted. "What happened? We almost crashed on the rocks!"

Buck did not reply.

Nate took over the tiller and headed the *Varmint* back out to sea. By the time the sun came up, Government Cut, the channel leading into Coral Gables, was visible. The storm had passed and they had no trouble sailing in. At the dock two customs officials boarded the boat, made sure that Nate Truman's ownership papers were in order, looked over everyone's identification, and inspected below.

Woman in the storm

"Tuviste alguna dificultad?" one of the officials asked, to which Manuel replied, "Nada. Todo estaba tranquilo."

When Roy and his uncle were in Buck's car headed west on Alligator Alley, Roy asked him, "Why did Manuel tell the customs officers that we had no difficulties?"

Buck lit a cigar, threw the match out the driver's side window, and said, "That's what they wanted to hear, so there were no more papers they'd have to fill out."

Roy wanted to ask his uncle how it was that he hadn't seen the tree but he did not. A year later, in a letter to Roy, who was in Chicago, Buck told him, "During the storm, in the darkness, I didn't see a tree. I saw a woman in a torn white dress, without arms, long black hair coiled around her head and body like snakes. Her mouth was open as if she was saying something, but because of the wind I couldn't hear her, then you brought the boat about. I didn't say anything at the time because I couldn't, I didn't understand what I had seen. It was a woman, I didn't recognize her. Manuel had seen her, too, but he told me later in Honduras that he'd been too frightened to tell you or Nate. He said he'd seen her again several times in dreams. I heard a couple of weeks ago that the *Varmint* cracked up and sank while Nate was attempting to sail from Nassau to Brazil. As far as the man who told me knew, none of the crew were lost."

Incurable

"Your father was a very generous man. He'd give you the shirt off his back, if he liked you. But in business he was tough, even ruthless; nobody got the better of him. Your mother shouldn't have divorced him; but then she shouldn't have married him, either."

Roy and his Uncle Buck, his mother's brother, were riding in Buck's Cadillac convertible on Dale Mabry Boulevard in Tampa, Florida, having just inspected a prospective site for a housing project Buck's company, Gulf Construction, was considering for development. Roy was thirteen years old; his father had been dead for almost two years. Since his parents had divorced when Roy was five, he had not known his father as well as he would have liked. During most of his childhood, Buck had been the primary paternal figure and influence in Roy's life.

"Were you and my dad friends?"

"We were friendly. He was only one year older but he had been in business since he was very young, so he was more experienced. I was just getting started as a civil engineer when your mother married him; and then for the first two years they were together I was up in the Yukon building the railroad. He knew most of the important people in Chicago, he made a good living. Your father made sure your mother had whatever she wanted and she enjoyed the nightlife. He was a twenty-four-hour kind of guy."

"He was much older than my mother."

"Fifteen years older. He was good to her, and he really loved you."

"Why didn't Nanny like him?"

"Your grandmother didn't dislike him, Roy. She was just protective of your mother. She was afraid of some of the people your dad did business with."

"I met a lot of those guys. They were nice to me."

"Why shouldn't they have been? You were a little boy and nobody wanted to get on the wrong side of your father."

"Nanny said they were dangerous."

"Even after your parents were divorced, if my mother had a problem she called your dad."

"Did he always fix it?"

"He loved your mother, so I'm sure he did what he could."

"I remember once when a guy my mother didn't want to see any more kept calling her and coming around, and Nanny said to her, 'If you don't call Rudy to take care of him, I will.' "

"There's a good Cuban place up here, La Teresita. Feel like eating?"

"Sure."

Buck pulled the Caddy into the parking lot of the restaurant. The sun was going down and when they got out of the car a strong breeze was blowing in off the Gulf.

"Just a minute, Roy. I'm going to put up the top in case it rains."

"I'll do it, Unk."

Roy slid into the driver's seat, turned the key in the ignition, and pushed the button that controlled the top. Once it was up, he fastened both the driver's and passenger's sides, turned the key off, removed it, got out, and handed the key to his uncle. The wind felt good and Roy stood still for a moment watching the sky turn different shades of red. This was one of the best things about Florida, he thought, the sunsets.

His mother had had three husbands since she divorced his father. Roy felt better when he was with his uncle. They went fishing together and Roy worked on construction jobs for him. Buck taught him about navigation, mineralogy, the correct way to build a staircase, and the architecture of bridges. He treated Roy differently than he did other men, not exactly as an equal, but Roy felt that he could trust him, that he could talk to his uncle about almost anything.

"I don't think I'll ever get married," Roy said.

Buck's first wife had divorced him and Roy knew that his uncle's second marriage was on the rocks.

" 'Weak you will find it in one only part, now pierced by love's incurable dart.' "

"What's that?"

"Lines from a sonnet by John Milton. I had to memorize it when I was in high school. Do you remember Rameses Thompson, who used to work for me?"

"The black guy who had a holster for his handgun on the inside of the driver's-side door of his pickup truck. Is he still around?"

"No. He killed his common-law wife, Rosita, and her girlfriend."

"His wife had a girlfriend?"

"They were stepsisters, from Panama City. Thompson got caught in Mobile, Alabama, and a cop shot him in his spine. I hear he's alive but can't use his arms or legs."

"He was very strong. He could lift two chairs at the same time holding each one by only one leg."

"Rosita was ugly and lazy, but Thompson was crazy about her."

Another thing Roy liked about the west coast of Florida was that rain was never far away. It started a few minutes after he and his uncle were inside La Teresita.

Three-Day Pass

I met Revancha Ríos in Mexico City in November of 1934. I'd been in Texas training to be a pilot for the navy. I had a three-day pass so a buddy and I decided to go to Mexico, where neither of us had ever been. We hopped a cheap flight from San Antonio and as soon as we got to Mexico City we hit the bars in the Centro Historico and Zona Rosa. We lost track of each other that first night and weren't together again until our flight back.

Being in our early twenties, we were both looking for girls to have a good time with. Frank hooked up with a couple of Americans, GIs, and went with them to a dance club they'd heard about. I had my eye on a very pretty girl who was sitting at a table with three other girls and two men in a restaurant and bar where Frank and I had eaten dinner, so I stuck around to see if I could talk to her.

I was standing at the bar and caught her eye. I smiled at her but she looked away. Just as I was thinking of going off to join Frank and the others at the dance club, the girl got up from the table, came over to me, and said, "Usted es solo?" I didn't speak much Spanish then but I understood that she asked me if I was alone. I said, "Sí, y usted?" She glanced at the people she'd been sitting with and said, "Yo soy ahora." I am now. She picked up off the bar the glass I'd been drinking from, drank what little was left in it, then asked me in English if I desired company.

For the next two days I couldn't get enough of Revancha Ríos.

I stayed with her in her tiny apartment in Roma Norte, ate and drank in places in that district, and made love the rest of the time. She didn't ask me many questions. I told her my name, that I was stationed in San Antonio, that I was from Chicago, that's about all. Revancha didn't offer much information about herself, either, only that she had always lived in Mexico City and that she was the youngest of six sisters. I paid for our meals and drinks, she never asked me for money. She dressed modestly and did not flirt with other men. On the second night she told me that she had a five-year-old son who lived with her mother, that she had been sixteen when he was born.

Before I left for the airport I gave Revancha almost all of the cash I had, about a hundred and twenty dollars. She drew a picture of herself on a piece of paper, folded it in half, and put it in one of my shirt pockets. That was more than thirty years ago. I still have it.

Figuring It Out

"I've got to get out of town for a while, nephew. You stay on at the house and keep working with Kip on the townhouse project."

"Where are you going, Unk?"

"Georgia. Don't tell anyone. An old girlfriend of mine and her husband live in Decatur. I'll bunk with them until things here are taken care of. Shouldn't be more than a week or two."

Roy's cousin Kip, Buck's son, had told him that the Tampa police suspected his father of being behind the torching of a building in Ybor City that Buck owned. A charge of arson had been filed by the insurance company which was refusing to pay Buck's claim.

Roy was fourteen years old; he lived in Chicago but was spending the summer with his uncle and working for his construction company. Kip was twenty-two and lived with his seventeen-year-old wife, Shayne.

"Here's some cash to hold you until I get back," said Buck, as he handed his nephew two hundred dollars.

They were alone in the Gulf Construction Company office. A 1959 calendar with a photograph of a dancing girl at the Tropicana nightclub in Havana was tacked to the wall behind Buck's desk. The day's date, July 16, was circled in red.

"Kip can handle the business, Roy. I'll give you a call at the house when I can. Elmer tells me the work at the townhouse is going well."

"We're going to set the trusses on the roof of 1612 day after tomorrow."

"Elmer's a good man. Just do what he says."

"I've watched him do more with one arm than any of the other guys on the job can do with two. How did he lose his left arm, Unk? In Korea?"

Buck grinned. "No. Husband of a lady Elmer was visiting blew it off with a shotgun. Don't ask him about it."

While Buck was away, Roy and Kip worked under Elmer's supervision and got the job done on 1612, then moved on to 1615. Two weeks stretched into three before Roy heard from his uncle.

"Are you still in Georgia, Unk?"

"Close enough. Elmer says you're holding your own."

"Trying to. We're on 1615 now. The staircase is almost finished. When are you coming back?"

"Any day now. I think we've got the insurance company about straightened out."

"Elmer said something funny the other day. He was carrying a concrete block on top of his right shoulder and I asked him how he'd hoisted it up there. He said, 'Only takes one steady hand to hold your pecker or light a match.' "

"Has he been drinking?"

"Not that I can tell."

"How are Kip and Shayne doing?"

"She came by the job about a week ago and told Kip she was going to stay with her mother in Fort Lauderdale. Kip called her a whore, then she drove off."

"Well, they'll either figure it out or they won't. Hang in there, Roy. Hasta pronto."

After Buck returned he didn't say anything to Roy about the fire or the charge of insurance fraud so Roy didn't ask him about it. Kip left for Fort Lauderdale to try to get Shayne to come back.

“I told Kip she was too young to get married,” Buck said. “For that matter, so was Kip.”

“Elmer says women never get over being young. What does he mean by that, Unk?”

“Don’t listen to what Elmer says about women. He’s lucky he still has his other arm.”

Fun Girl

"You remember Rameses Thompson?"

"Sure. He used to collect rents for you and drove with you to Honduras."

"He's paralyzed now."

"You told me. His girlfriend shot him in the back."

"His mother, Lucy, died in the North Carolina State Hospital for Negro Insane, in Goldsboro, near Raleigh. Rameses called me yesterday and asked me if I would go there and arrange to have her body shipped down to Mobile, where he lives. You want to ride up with me?"

It was early December, 1962. Roy was fifteen. He'd flown down from Chicago, where he lived with his mother and her third husband, whom he didn't like, to spend the holidays with his Uncle Buck in Tampa, Florida.

"All right. How long will we be gone?"

"Three days, I figure. Maybe four. We'll be back in plenty of time for Christmas."

Roy liked keeping company with Buck, listening to his stories and learning how to do things he'd never done. His uncle had lived an adventurous life, traveling all over the world, working as a civil and mechanical engineer as well as an architect, building bridges and railroads and houses. His second wife, Carmen, was from Madrid, Spain, where Buck had met and married her, then taken her to the States. They'd lived for a few years in Chicago before moving to Florida. They had one child, a daughter, who was five years old.

The trip to North Carolina in Buck's Cadillac Eldorado was uneventful, and he took care of the shipping costs for Lucy Thompson's remains to Mobile, Alabama, as a favor to her son. On their way back to Tampa, however, Roy's uncle decided to make a stop in Atlanta, Georgia, to look up a woman he told Roy he had not seen in three years.

"Her name is Shirley Cousins, or at least it was when I knew her. I used to run around with her once in a while. She and her husband—Ed, I think his name was—lived in Tampa then, in a house I built off 30th Street across from Busch Gardens. He got arrested for counterfeiting and passing funny money and had to do time, during which Shirley divorced him. She sold the house and went to stay with her sister in Atlanta. Shirley wrote me from there so I visited her once. Smart girl, attractive, had a good figure, but kind of a hustler. She told me she had two men on the line, both supporting her."

"Did they know about each other?"

"Of course not. Shirley knows how to juggle men. She claimed she had a daughter or son at boarding school and a mother in Memphis she had to support, but she didn't have a child and her mother was dead."

"What about her sister?"

"I never met her. In fact, I don't know if she really has a sister."

"Are you sure you want to see her, Unk? She sounds awful shady. And I'll be in the way."

"I'm just curious. Don't worry, Roy, you won't be in the way."

Buck remembered where Shirley's apartment was—in Decatur, a town within the city limits of Atlanta—parked in front, and told Roy to wait in the car while he went into the building to see if Shirley still lived there. Ten minutes later, Buck came out and got back into the car.

"Did you see her?" Roy asked.

"No, the apartment house manager told me that Shirley was murdered a year ago by her ex-husband, who then hanged himself in the apartment. Too bad, Shirley could be a fun girl when she wanted to be."

"What about her sister?"

"The manager said he didn't know anything about a sister."

The Dolphins

Roy's Uncle Buck built a house on Utila, one of the Bay Islands of Honduras. It was an octagonal structure with eight doors on a spit of land accessible only by boat when the tide was in. Buck had transported a generator, refrigerator, and other appliances on the ship *Islander Trader* from St. Petersburg, Florida, to Utila, and when he returned on the same boat two and a half months later, Roy met him at the dock.

"I had to go to Teguci for a few days to renew my residency visa and take care of some other business," Buck told him, "and I was walking down a street with my friend Goodnight Morgan, who used to live on Utila but now lives on Roatan, when a car came by, slowed down, and someone fired three shots at us, then sped away. Neither of us were hit. Drive-bys are common in Tegucigalpa, it's the murder capital of Latin America, if not the world, but I didn't know why anyone would want to kill us. Goodnight Morgan used to be High Sheriff of Utila, so I asked him if he thought he could have been targeted by a political rival or a criminal who held a grudge against him. Goodnight said either was possible, but he didn't think so. 'Gangsters in Teguci kill for no reason other than to intimidate the population,' he said. 'That's why almost nobody is on the streets. To shop they go to malls where there are security guards with automatic weapons to protect them.' "

Roy and his uncle were driving on the bridge over the bay on their way to Tampa when Buck said, "The *Islander Trader* started leaking fuel when we were a day from port, and the radio was on the fritz. We barely made it to Roatan. The leak had to be patched up before going on to Utila. Then came the shooting in Teguci. Keep in mind, nephew, when a person walks out the door you might never see him or her again."

It was a hot and humid day, which was not unusual, but the exceptionally heavy cloud cover, without wind, portended rain, at the very least.

"This weather reminds me of the time I was in Callao, waiting for a ship to take me to Panama City, where I could get a plane to Miami," said Buck. "Hundreds of dolphins invaded the harbor, making it impossible for boats to get in or out. They sensed that a giant storm was coming and they were trying to get out of its way. I'll never forget the sight of those blue-green dolphins crowded together like cattle in the stockyards in Chicago. Dolphins are big, the adults average seven feet long, and they were jabbering to each other, loud, squealing and honking that drowned out everything else."

"Did a big storm hit?"

"About four hours later, the rain started, then huge waves inundated the Peruvian coast, followed by a hailstorm, the kind you get in Kansas or Oklahoma. Nobody there had even seen hail before. All of the ships tied up or at anchor in and near the harbor were damaged, and a number of boats out at sea capsized."

"What about the dolphins?"

"They dove deeper to avoid the hail. But when the bad weather passed, the dolphins were all gone, no sight or sound of them. They were already miles away in the Pacific."

"How long were you stuck in Callao?"

"About a week. I went to Lima for a couple of days, then went back to get my ship."

Rain hit the windshield, so Roy slowed the car down. They were almost across the bridge.

"Dolphins are smart, Roy, they know when and how to escape from the weather and other cetaceans. Human beings are the biggest threat to their existence. I told Goodnight Morgan about the dolphins in Callao, and you know what he said?"

Roy shook his head.

"That's why you never see any dolphins walking down the street in Tegucigalpa."

The Racket

When I brought my second wife, Carmen, to America for the first time, in 1956, just after we were married, we crossed the ocean from Le Havre to New York on the Queen Mary.

We were in first class and on the evening of our second day at sea we were in the bar when I saw the writer Ernest Hemingway and his wife—his fourth—Mary seated at a corner table. Actually, it was Carmen who recognized him and pointed him out to me. Carmen and I were standing at the end of the bar closest to the Hemingways' table. A few minutes later, he looked at me and waved a hand, motioning for me to come over. I was surprised, of course, but I walked over and he spoke to me in Spanish.

Carmen

He addressed me as Arturo and asked what I was doing on the ship. I replied, also in Spanish, that my name was not Arturo, identified myself, and said that my wife and I were returning to our home in Chicago. Hemingway smiled and, in English, said he had mistaken me for an acquaintance of his from Cuba, where he lived.

"Is that your wife?" he asked, nodding toward Carmen. I said it was and he told me to bring her over. I did and he invited us to sit down in the two empty chairs at their table.

"I'm from Chicago originally," he said, "Oak Park. Live in Havana now."

He introduced me to Mary and I introduced Carmen. We joined them and Carmen mentioned that she was from Madrid, though she had been born and mostly raised in Paris. Hemingway said that he had spent a considerable amount of time in both cities. He asked me what my profession was and I told him that I was a civil engineer and builder. He wanted to know if I had been in the war. I said I had, that I'd been a lieutenant commander in the navy. He ordered drinks for all of us and insisted that we call him Ernest.

Mary told us that she was a journalist, that during the war she had been a correspondent for various magazines stationed in France and England. When Carmen told them that she was a singer, Hemingway suggested that she sing something, so she gave them a bit of "Siboney," after which both Ernest and Mary applauded, as did several of the other patrons in the bar. At this point our wives began a conversation—in French—and Ernest and I stood up and went over to the bar to replenish our drinks.

"Tell me, Buck, what's Chicago like these days?" he asked. "I haven't been there for thirty years. Before locating myself in Cuba with my third wife, Martha, I lived in Key West."

I told him that Carmen and I were planning to move soon to Florida, Tampa to be exact, which has a large Cuban population. There were more building opportunities there, I explained, no state income taxes, and better weather.

"I never could bear the weather in Chicago," he said, "too cold in the winter, too hot and humid in the summer. I don't like to have to wear a lot of clothes. I feel best when I'm on my boat in the Gulf Stream. Do you fish?"

I said I did and added that I kept a sailboat at the Columbia Yacht Club.

"Do you read much?" he asked. "I mean other than newspapers

and magazines and materials pertaining to the construction business."

I asked him if he meant novels.

He nodded and asked, "Who are your favorite writers?"

I told him that I didn't have as much time to read as I'd like to, but that I had read his novel *For Whom the Bell Tolls*.

"What did you think?" Ernest asked.

I told him that it reads like a translation from the Spanish, which increases the verisimilitude.

Hemingway laughed out loud, clapped me hard on one of my shoulders, and said, "That's the finest compliment you could have given me, Colby. Maybe you're in the wrong racket. From now until we get to New York your bar bill is on me. Let's go see if we can get your lovely wife to sing another Cuban song."

"Maybe you're in the wrong racket."

Ernest Hemingway

A Good Place to Get Married

"When I get up in the morning and go into the bathroom to shave, I look in the mirror and say, 'Who is that guy?' "

Buck told this to his fifteen-year-old nephew, Roy, when Buck was in his fifties. He would go on to live for forty more years. Buck said this a year after his father, Roy's grandfather, died at the age of eighty-two. After having lived most of his life in Chicago, Buck and his second wife, Carmen, had moved to Tampa, Florida, where he established a construction business, building tract houses. Buck was a handsome man, he was vain, and since his early twenties had been what was commonly referred to as a ladies' man. He had occasional girlfriends while he was married but nothing really serious until he began seeing Maureen on a regular basis.

Maureen was a divorcée in her late thirties who lived with her eighteen-year-old daughter in one of the tract houses built by Buck's company. She was an attractive tall blonde who took courses in art and philosophy at the University of South Florida and was a serious painter. Buck took her on trips out of the country, most often to Honduras, where Buck kept a house on the Bay Island of Utila. Maureen enjoyed windsurfing there, even in shark-infested waters, and doing oil paintings of local people and places. Buck was impressed by her artistic talent and fearless athleticism. A year after their relationship began, Maureen prevailed upon Buck to marry her in Roatan, the capital of the Bay

Islands. "We'll just be married in Honduras," Maureen said. "You can keep Carmen in Tampa." Buck did not take this marriage seriously and did not tell anyone about it.

There came a time when Maureen requested that Buck financially support both her and her daughter, who had psychological problems which required regular medical care. Buck had never minded giving Maureen money on occasion, but he balked at this demand. Maureen threatened to reveal their liaison to Carmen and, if necessary, to sue him for alimony. Buck informed Maureen that their Honduran marriage would not be recognized legally in Florida, and therefore he owed her nothing.

Maureen consulted the attorney she had used for her previous divorce; he explained that she had no legal rights but could sue Buck for breach of promise, though that would be determined on a basis of her word against his. The attorney added that her chances in court of achieving financial satisfaction were not good. The best thing for Maureen to do, he suggested, would be for her to prevail upon Buck to settle their situation privately, if possible without rancor.

When Roy, who had met Maureen and liked her, asked his uncle why he didn't see her any more, Buck told him what had happened and said, "Don't ever expect relationships, either personal or professional, to end well, especially when money is involved."

"Did you have to pay off Maureen?" Roy asked.

"I gave her a little something. She wasn't happy with the amount, but she took it."

"What about in Honduras?"

"What about Honduras?"

"You're still married to Maureen there, aren't you?"

"In Roatan, all a man has to do to get rid of his wife is to pay a judge fifty dollars to declare a marriage null and void on the basis of incompatibility."

"What if they have children?"

"The same. It's up to the man if he wants to pay child support."

"I guess it's better to be a man in Honduras."

"Yes, nephew, it's a good place to get married."

"I'll remember that, Unk."

"I'll tell you a story about Maureen. She wanted to go to Paris, so I took her there. We flew first class both ways. The first thing she wanted to see was the Eiffel Tower. We went all the way to the top. We stayed at a swanky hotel, went to all of the art museums, the best restaurants. I hired a car and took her to Versailles to visit the palace. After we got back to Tampa her friend Agnes told me that Maureen complained to her about how I rushed her around Paris, only stayed a week, said I needed to get back to oversee a building project. Maureen told Agnes that she knew I couldn't cover up a longer absence to Carmen. She even said I left her alone one night for two hours so I could go with a prostitute. Maureen and I were never apart the whole time."

"Did you go to Paris with Maureen before or after you married her in Honduras?"

"After."

"So it was like a honeymoon."

"I suppose she thought of it like that."

Roy did not ask his uncle about Maureen again, but one night when they went for dinner at a restaurant they saw her sitting at a table with a man. Maureen saw them, too, but pretended she hadn't.

Incompleteness

Roy's Uncle Buck was a conservative gambler. When he played poker on Wednesday nights in a regular game with his cronies in Tampa, Florida, in the late 1950s and 1960s, he strictly followed the rules set forth in John Scarne's bible, sticking to the odds, rarely losing, mostly winning a little.

In 1960, when he was fifteen, Roy accompanied his uncle on a gambling junket to Mamba Cay in the Bahamas. Buck was a civil and mechanical engineer, well-schooled in higher mathematics, who had established a construction business, building houses and shopping malls throughout Florida. He was in his early fifties when he and Roy went to Mamba Cay. Buck also took with him a hooker in her twenties named Gina, an attractive blonde with a slim figure who spoke with a pronounced lisp. On the charter flight out of Tampa, while Buck was dozing, she told Roy she was looking forward to doing a little business on the island.

"What about my uncle?" Roy asked her. "I think he expects you to stick exclusively with him."

Gina smiled and nodded. "I'll give him what he needs. He's an easy man to satisfy."

When she said the word satisfy it came out "Thatithfy."

Buck, Gina, and Roy were among a dozen or so Floridians on this excursion conducted by Cash'n'Splash Tours. The person in charge of the group was Bill Leach, a bald, obese, cockeyed man in his mid-sixties wearing a tan leisure suit and flat-topped Panama hat. He shook everyone's hand and assured them they were going to have "a super-duper time."

Gina scoped out the men standing on the tarmac waiting to board the plane and said to Roy, "Another girl and I could handle them all in a couple of hours. Fast fingers and a little lip ticklin', the bunch."

"What if they're drunk?"

"It don't matter, honey, they just want what their wives won't give 'em and probably never done more'n once."

The junketeers were given simply furnished, spacious rooms in the Prince Mamba Arms Hotel. Buck and Gina had their own room and Roy was to share a room with Bill Leach. The casino was in the hotel; meals, the cost of which, except for alcoholic drinks, was included in the package, were to be taken either in the Mamba Bar Lounge or the Prince and Princess Mamba Dining Room.

Roy asked Leach who the Prince and Princess Mamba were.

"Never asked, myself. Hotel has a little history in their brochure about some kinda slave rebellion. They got it at the desk."

Bill Leach handed Roy a room key and told him to get settled in.

"Got me my own place, son, on the other side of the island, if you get my drift. I'll catch up with everyone later in the casino."

Roy did not see him again until three days later when the group met for the flight back to Tampa.

Roy asked his uncle if he would be allowed to gamble in the casino.

"If anyone asks how old you are," said Buck, "tell them you're eighteen. How much money do you have?"

"About forty dollars."

"Here's forty more. Stick with roulette. Wait until the red comes up twice in a row, then bet the next four times on the black. You can reverse it, too. Don't bet numbers, the wheels have double zeros."

"What're you gonna play, Unk?"

"Blackjack, poker, craps."

That night Roy followed Buck's instructions, then caught up with him at the craps table.

"How'd you do?" Buck asked.

"I'm ahead twenty-two dollars."

"Did anyone ask your age?"

"No."

"The only bets you want to make here are against shooters trying to make their points. Always bet on their first rolls, then lay out until the shooter rolls a seven or eleven, makes their point or craps out."

"What if you're throwing the dice?"

Buck laughed. "Use your best judgment."

Roy spotted Gina in the casino early on, then not again until three or four hours later when she came into the Mamba Bar and slid onto a stool next to Roy's.

"What's your poison, fella?"

"Ginger ale."

"You got enough money left to buy a girl a rum punch? If not, I'll buy you one."

"I can pay, but you'll have to order. The bartender asked to see my ID."

"A rum punch," Gina told the bartender, whose name tag read Amos Mamba.

When he brought her drink Gina asked him, "Mamba really your last name?"

"No. Every employee of the hotel uses it. The management wants us to feel like we're part of the same family."

"Do you?"

"Ten dollars," he said.

Gina put a twenty on the bar, then said to Roy, "I'm rich tonight."

The bartender stared at her.

"Keep the change, Amos," she said.

"Amos Williams," he said, and walked away.

"I didn't see you at the tables," said Roy.

"I'll go in in a minute and see how your uncle's doin'. How about you?"

"I won a little, then lost back most of what I'd won. Where've you been?"

"Like I told you, playin' my own game."

"Does my uncle know?"

"He might suspect somethin', but long as I keep myself available to him he won't complain."

Gina picked up her drink, slid off the stool, then brushed her vermilion lips against Roy's left cheek.

Amos Williams came over and watched her walk toward the casino.

"How you know her?" he asked.

"She's my mother," said Roy.

The next day Roy spent at the hotel pool, swimming and relaxing in the sun. Gina joined him, took a dip, then fell asleep in the lounge chair nearest his. Again that evening she appeared briefly in the casino. Roy did not see her leave.

On their third and last day, at four o'clock in the afternoon, Buck asked Roy, who was sitting on the edge of the pool, if he'd seen Gina.

"No, Unk. Not since early last night in the casino. Are you ahead?"

"Down two grand. I'll make it up tonight. See you at dinner."

Neither Roy's uncle nor Gina appeared in the restaurant that evening. Roy saw Buck shooting craps later but did not approach him. He did not see him again until noon the following day when the Cash'n'Splash group convened in the hotel lobby before boarding a bus to the airport.

"Hi, Unk. Where's Gina?"

"She didn't come back last night. I don't know where she is."

Bill Leach entered the lobby for the first time in three days and went around smiling and asking everyone if they had enjoyed themselves. He was wearing a powder-blue leisure suit. A taxi stopped in front of the hotel and Gina got out. She rushed past Buck and Roy, saying only, "I've got to get my things."

On the bus and then on the plane Gina sat next to Bill Leach. Roy's uncle made no attempt to speak with her. At the Tampa airport Gina stuck next to Bill Leach, picked up her suitcase at the baggage claim, waved at Roy, and headed for the taxi stand.

"How did you come out, Unk? Did you make up the two grand?"

Buck did not reply to Roy until after they had retrieved their bags and left the terminal. They deposited the suitcases in the trunk of Buck's 1959 Continental, he closed it and looked around. He hadn't said anything since he'd ordered a drink on the plane.

"Roy, even if you know what the odds are there's no way you can be absolutely certain what will happen. The black or red can come up forty times in a row or not at all. You can consecutively roll seven or eleven a dozen times or more, or, theoretically, never again. Inevitability is random. The real question has to do with incompleteness, to accept that something is not or cannot be completed. For centuries physicists and philosophers have struggled and argued about this without arriving at a satisfactory explanation or conclusion."

Buck looked at his nephew, smiled, and said, "No, Roy, not only did I not make up the two grand, I lost three more. That's the only thing I'm certain of. Did you have a good time?"

Roy thought about Gina. "Thatithfactory," she would have said.

Castor and Pollux in America

Roy met Trick Mullvaney in 1962, a couple of months after Trick got out of prison. Trick, whose Christian name was Patrick, was paroled to the custody of Roy's Uncle Buck, who provided him a construction job in Tampa, Florida, where Buck lived. Roy was fifteen at the time, Trick was twenty-two, the same age as Buck's son, Kip, who introduced them. Trick knew Kip from before he was sent to Raiford for stealing medical supplies—narcotics, mostly—from pharmacies in Hillsborough County. Kip persuaded his father to take a chance on Trick, which required Buck to sponsor and keep track of him for one year, the length of his parole. Roy's uncle rented an apartment for Trick on a property he owned near the construction site Trick worked on with Kip, building townhouses north of Tampa in Temple Terrace. Kip and Roy, when he was visiting from Chicago for the summer, lived with Buck and his wife, Belita, Kip's stepmother.

Trick took his wife, Lorelei, and their four-year-old daughter, Tanya, to live with him. Trick was good-looking, tall and lean, fair-haired, and had a Van Dyke beard he began growing as soon as he was released from "durance vile," as Buck referred to imprisonment. Roy's uncle had had a taste of it himself when he'd been in the marines, having spent four months in the brig for bringing girls into the barracks to service the men. He had been spared a dishonorable discharge thanks to his father bribing a congressman he had helped to get elected.

"Raiford isn't so bad," Trick told Kip and Roy, "compared to local and county lockups. Negroes do all the dirty work, of course, this being the South. Shouldn't be that way, but state prisons in the North aren't much different. They're segregated, too, even in New Hampshire, where I grew up."

The boys were sitting and drinking beer in Trick and Lorelei's living room after work. Roy was also on the job, shovelling lime rock off the curbs where Buck's construction company was paving streets.

"Can't be fun, huh, Roy?" Trick said. "Hundred and some out there every day, hotter when those trucks come through shootin' asphalt. How much is your uncle paying you?"

"A dollar an hour."

"Negroes get eighty-five cents," said Kip.

"It's not right," Lorelei said. "What if they have families? That's not a living wage."

Trick laughed. "In Raiford all the inmates get paid the same, nine cents an hour. Don't go to prison, Roy, no matter what state you're in."

"Roy won't never do a jolt," said Kip. "He's too smart, he'll go to college. Isn't that right, cousin?"

"I'm goin' to college after I'm off parole," said Trick, "then maybe divinity school. I got tight with a parson in Raiford. He'd had a good life, he told me, until he got caught puttin' it to an eleven-year-old girl. Couldn't keep his hands and other body parts off underage poontang. Roscoe Rainwater. There he was in a North Florida swamp with me layin' sewer pipe instead of little girls. Told me he quoted scripture all the while he was taking his pleasure."

"Quit, Patrick!" said Lorelei. "No more trashy jailhouse stories. I don't want Tanya to ever know you were in prison."

"You're right, honey, I've got to fight to keep my mind clean, but it's damn sure hard work."

"Do you like living in Chicago, Roy?" Lorelei asked. "What do your parents do?"

"My father's dead and my mother gets married."

"He was only five when his dad died," said Kip. "And his mother's been married three times since."

"Jesus on a pony," said Trick. "Ain't life grand?"

"It will be for Tanya," said Lorelei.

"I'll do my best to make that happen, darlin'," Trick said. "If I don't, promise you'll shoot me."

Lorelei looked directly into her husband's eyes when she said, "I promise."

Trick maintained his good behavior during the year he worked for Roy's uncle, and after his term of parole ended he passed a high school equivalency examination and enrolled in the University of South Florida in Tampa. He did passably well there and two years later entered the Pontius Pilate School of Divine Investigation in nearby Boca Lupo, from which he earned a certificate entitling him to call himself a Doctor of Divine Investigation and proselytize wheresoever God directed him to go.

Kip, meanwhile, had a falling out with his father over a navy insurance policy Kip wanted Buck to sign over to him and moved to Las Vegas, Nevada, where he became a card dealer. He worked there in various casinos for a few years but became an alcoholic. His alcoholism caused him to be fired repeatedly until he was no longer employable in Vegas. He bounced around the country, working as a taxi driver in Denver, an elevator operator in Chicago, a janitor in Kansas City, and a fruit picker in Texas.

During all of this time Kip and Trick Mullvaney stayed in touch by mail and occasional phone calls. Trick and Lorelei started a church in Boulder, Colorado, where they bought a big house on a mountainside with money Lorelei inherited from her parents following their deaths in an automobile accident. Tanya graduated from the University of Colorado with a degree in engineering, after which she moved to Montana.

Trick proved himself successful as a pastor but soon fell prey to what he referred to as Roscoe Rainwater Syndrome, which caused his downfall. After losing the majority of his parishioners, he began playing the stock market with the remainder of Lorelei's inheritance, eventually losing it all. Their house was foreclosed upon and his Church of Divine Wrath and Retribution was shuttered. Lorelei filed for divorce and went to live with Tanya in Montana, where Tanya worked as a civil engineer in the city of Bozeman. Lorelei never again spoke to Trick, shed the name Mullvaney, and soon remarried to a local real estate salesman named Ripley Palmer. Tanya refused to answer her father's letters or take his phone calls, ignoring his repeated requests that she send him money. She married a firefighter who threatened to murder Trick if he did not cease trying to contact Tanya.

Trick returned to Tampa, where, like Kip in Denver, he became a taxi driver. The Pontius Pilate School of Divine Investigation had closed due to its founder, Franklin Furto, having been convicted of defrauding several businessmen who had been on the school's board of directors. He was sentenced to serve fifteen years in the state prison at Raiford, which gave Trick a chuckle. Trick lost his looks and drank himself to death at the age of forty-two, not long before Kip, depressed and destitute, shot himself in the head while sitting on the steps of the entrance to a fast food restaurant in Phoenix, Arizona.

Roy, who never did go to college, nevertheless traveled the world and became a successful author of popular adventure novels for boys. He lived in Santa Fe, New Mexico, and corresponded frequently with his Uncle Buck, who informed Roy of Trick's early demise and his son Kip's suicide. Buck outlived both of them, passing away in his sleep at the age of ninety-three.

Roy was troubled and mystified by the facts of how his cousin Kip and Kip's pal Trick Mullvaney had led such pathetic lives and come to terrible, if not tragic, ends. When Roy was fifteen, they had been kind to him, generous with the little money they had, did their best to keep him out of trouble and harm's way, and always welcomed his company. Roy decided to write a novel about two young friends named Trick and Kip and their often humorous adventures and misadventures together. He would make everything up.

Trick Mullvaney

The Good Listener

Roy's Uncle Buck and his friend Tony Grimaldi, who owned the Abeja Bank in Ybor City, played poker with two or three other men on Thursday nights. This was in the 1960s when Tampa, Florida, was still a relatively small city, a shrimp and cigar town, as Grimaldi called it. Ybor City was the center of the Cuban American community, which it had been since the mid-nineteenth century. Tony Grimaldi wasn't Cuban but, having grown up there, spoke Spanish like one.

"C'mon, Gus, you want cards or not?"

"Tony, you know how much time it takes you to okay or refuse a loan?"

"No time. You need a loan or cards?"

"One."

"Buck?"

"I'm good."

"Art?"

"Dos."

"Ralph?"

"I'm out."

"Speakin' of loans?"

"Art?"

"What about Don Kay? You know he's goin' away for torchin' the Riviera Terrace."

"Don Kay don't worry me. You worry me, always takin' two cards."

Buck, Art, Tony, and Gus showed their hands. Buck scraped up the pot. After the game ended and only Tony and Buck were still seated at the table, Buck asked Tony about Sam Lowiski.

"He's in Dallas with that puta, the counterfeit rubia makes stag films."

"You like her, Tony, don't you?"

Tony lit a Chesterfield, puffed on it a few times, then said, "Mary Duckworth is her real name."

"Lowiski calls her Deronda LeMay. Anyhow, he come through?"

Grimaldi stubbed out his cigarette.

"I could use another beer."

"Gus killed the last one."

"If he don't show by tomorrow, we'll go get him. I can send Izzy."

"You mean Lefty, whose left arm got shot off by that runt Martinelli?"

"Israel Izquierda, yeah."

"Funny he's called Lefty when it's his left arm's the one missing."

"To remind him be more cuidado how he goes about his business. Unless you want to go. We could drive up together Saturday."

"Can't. Taking my nephew fishing."

"Roy's a smart boy. How old's he now?"

"Twelve."

"Good you're there for him. His mother's still got her looks but she's a wreck."

"My sister's never recovered from the break-up of her second marriage. She had a nervous breakdown, plus she has a skin condition puts her in the hospital."

"You teachin' Roy the construction business?"

"He wants to be a writer."

Tony laughed. "He's just a kid, he needs to learn how to make a livin'. Writin' what?"

"Stories."

"I'll talk to him."

"He's got his own mind, like his father."

"When my old man died, I was fifteen," Tony said. "He was from Trapani, in Sicily. He had old country rules. They still apply."

Two days later, when Buck and Roy were on Buck's boat in the Gulf of Mexico, Buck said, "You ought to go see Tony Grimaldi, he likes you. You could get some good stories from him."

"I like Tony, too. He lets me sit in the chair behind his desk when I go in the bank. One thing I know already is that to be a writer it's important to be a good listener."

"Your dad had plenty of stories."

"He told me some things that happened in Romania when he was a boy, about people who lived in his village that believed in magic. There was an older boy who talked to pigs and the pigs talked to him. One of the pigs predicted everybody's future, how some of them would have accidents like falling off a roof or drowning when they were drunk, or being stabbed by their wife. But somehow the way my dad told the stories, even though the fortune-telling pig predicted someone being torn apart by wild dogs or run over by a train, they were funny. Those are the kinds of stories I want to write, funny tragedies. If death is the worst thing that can happen to a person but there's something funny about it then it might not be so bad. What do you think, Unk?"

"Well, I've seen men die with smiles on their faces. Not many, a few. When I was with the Seabees, stationed on an island in the South Pacific, Vanua Levu, we built Quonset huts to house the men. It was my idea, modeled on Narragansett tribal construction, that I studied in engineering school. One of the men fell off a ladder and broke his neck. He died, but not right away. His name was Bentley, from Alabama. Bentley asked me why we were building Quonset huts and I told him the Indians built them for protection from freezing cold winters. 'There's no winter here, Commander,' he said. I explained that the long, high ceilings not only kept heat in during the cold months but kept the temperature down in the hot months. 'The Indians figured that out, did they?' he asked. I said yes, in Rhode Island. 'My granny Calwallader was right,' Bentley said. I asked him what she was right about, and he said, 'If you got some curiosity in you, you can learn something new near every day.' Then Bentley died, smiling. Calwallader must have been his mother's family name."

"What do you think happens to a person after he dies?"

"Nothing. There's just no person anymore."

"Dead people live in other people's memories, Unk, like my dad. He'll always be there in my mind."

Years later, after Tony Grimaldi, Roy's Uncle Buck, and Roy's mother were dead, Roy refused to forget them. Instead, he wrote about them as they were, as he imagined they were, and as they never were or even could have been. He figured if he had known them as well as he thought he'd known them then what he wrote would be as close as he would ever come to the truth.

ENGINEERS - DESIGNERS - BUILDERS

FLORIDA STATE REGISTERED
PROFESSIONAL CIVIL ENGINEER

COLBY, P.E.

TAMPA, FLORIDA 33617

June 16, 19

Dear

Just got back from Mexico on the 13th. Needed a break from my drawing board - and had a great time there. Three years ago I met a man in Chelem and we were going to go fishing the next day - anyhow I broke my leg the "next" day and I couldn't phone him. So 3 years later I went to visit him and was overwhelmed with his courtesies. Stayed at his house and he and his wife treated me wonderfully. We went fishing in the small boat, with motor, four miles out in the gulf and caught a lot of grouper - which we later ate. Like he said "Anyone would think we were crazy to go way out in that sized boat". He had a lot of stories - where he capsized one time and swam 5 miles to shore. He said he took his time, floated and was lucky the wind was right. Never thought about drowning. Another time he was broken down way out anddrifted for three days without food or water. His wife and all had given him up for lost. Anyway, stayed a couple of days and the hotel staff in Progreso treated me as family. I really envy the life there and should have chosen Mexico in the first place.

Much more than a lot oflove to you all

How He Found Out

"You know a lot of people, Buck, all kinds of people."

"Yes. So?"

"I have a problem. My wife has been carrying on with a guy. She gives him money."

"How do you know?"

"She has access to my bank account. I make a regular deposit so I'm usually up to date on the balance. For several months now it's been short."

"You're sure she's supporting this person?"

"I don't know about supporting him but helping him out, anyway. The money's going somewhere. I assume it's to him."

"Cherchez la femme."

"What's that?"

"Look for the woman. A French expression. What do you want me to do about it?"

"Help me find out who this man is. I've tried, but no luck. I've confronted her about it but Martine just laughs at me, says there's nobody else, that she treats her girlfriends to lunch or dinner when I'm out of town."

"Are you often out of town?"

"On business. I own a steel company and it's necessary that I call on customers to look over their projects."

"I can recommend a private investigator."

"Is he trustworthy?"

"I've used her on occasion. Her rates are reasonable."

"Her?"

Buck nodded, wrote something on a piece of paper, stood up, and came around his desk and handed the paper to his visitor.

"Anita Ray," he said. "This is her phone number. She works from home."

"You think a woman . . . ?"

"Who better to figure out how a woman's mind works than another woman?"

"Okay, Buck, I'll give her a try. Thanks."

"Take care, Bill. Let me know how things work out."

Buck sat on the edge of his desk and thought about Bill's predicament. If this were his own problem Buck knew what he would do: close the bank account and move the funds somewhere else where his wife had no access to them. She would then have to come directly to him. What difference will it make for Bill to know who the benefactor is of his wife's largesse? The marriage is over; Bill will never trust her again.

About a month later Anita Ray called Buck. She thanked him for sending Bill to her.

"How did it go?" he asked.

"The first thing I did was tell him to close the bank account and require her to come to him for money."

"What was the second thing? Did you track down his wife's outside man?"

"Yes. Not a man, a woman."

"Bill must have been surprised."

"I suppose so, but the story was the same. The upshot was that the wife left him. Bill has filed for divorce."

"Nobody got shot."

"Somebody did."

"Who?"

"The girlfriend's girlfriend shot and killed the girlfriend."

"Crazy."

"Not so crazy. You know that French expression, don't you? Cherchez la femme."

"I mentioned it to Bill when he came to see me. He didn't know what it meant."

Anita laughed. "He does now," she said.

End of the World

After the end of World War II, in 1945, Buck was in Belfast, Ireland. He had not been there for almost ten years, when he was in the navy and working as an undercover agent for the Office of Strategic Services. Since his discharge from the service a year before, Buck had worked as a civil engineer on various jobs, designing and overseeing the construction of everything from bridges to shopping malls. He decided to take a break and revisit Ireland, where he had spent several enjoyable months. On his first afternoon in Belfast, he decided to step into the End of the World pub for a pint of Guinness. At the entrance he was greeted by a tall, burly middle-aged man, who said to him, "Aren't you Lieutenant Commander Colby? My name is Ferol Rooney, we met before the war, in Derry, at Mrs. O'Sullivan's boarding house."

Buck looked closely at the man's face.

"I'm sorry," Buck said, "but I don't recall our having met before. Not that we haven't, but I can't place you in Derry or elsewhere."

"Time and war will do that to a man. Look here, Commander, would you be in need of a pistol? I've one to flog, a relic of sorts, a Desert Eagle, in good working condition, taken off an Orangeman during The Troubles."

"No, thank you. I've no use for such a weapon."

"Well then, as the poet said, 'You know that there is no difference at all between that which you call good and evil, and that at the heart of each lies only suffering.' "

"I most certainly do, Mr. Rooney. Good day to you."

Feeling as if he were re-entering the world, Buck entered the End of the World.

Perils of Longevity

"Hola, sobrino, how are you?"

"Pretty good, Unk. How about you?"

"It will be my ninetieth birthday the day after tomorrow."

"I know, I was going to call you."

"I want you to know that I've revised my estimate of longevity. Remember I told you that life expectancy should be a hundred and twenty years?"

"Yes."

"According to my latest research, a normal lifespan, barring cataclysmic occurrence, should be one hundred and thirty."

"I'm happy to hear it."

"How old are you now, Roy?"

"Forty-five."

"Take care of yourself, nephew, you have eighty-five years to go."

"Do you have any plans for your birthday?"

"My friend Delilah is going to take me out for dinner, and she's baking me a cake."

"How old is Delilah?"

"Thirty-two."

"A little old for you, Unk."

"I know, but she looks younger. It's hard to believe that all of my old friends are dead."

"There's nothing you can do about that."

"It's a shame Kip couldn't have been more like you. He would have been forty-nine now. I wasn't a very good father."

"You did a lot for him, you were always generous and tried to help him whenever he got into trouble."

Roy could hear his uncle crying softly.

"I'll call you on your birthday, Unk, before you go out with Delilah."

"I love you, Roy."

"I love you, too, tio."

Roy's uncle hung up first. Roy thought about his cousin, Kip, his uncle's son from his first marriage, who had committed suicide three years before. Roy wondered why, following his parents' divorce when he was nineteen, Kip had always addressed his father by their last name.

The Chinese Shadow

Roy's Uncle Buck Colby, his mother's brother, was a world traveller, and three weeks before his ninety-third birthday he decided to go to Havana, Cuba. He had two homes, one on Utila in the Bay Islands of Honduras, and the other in Tampa, Florida. He had been to Cuba many times, beginning in the 1940s, but not for several years; he was curious to see for himself how things had changed, if at all, since Fidel Castro had died.

Buck went by himself, he was fluent in Spanish and remembered his way around Havana. He stayed at the National, in its day the most elegant hotel on the island, now a bit run down, but still redolent of older, better times. He walked around the city, dallied as much as he was capable of dallying with a few of the plentiful array of prostitutes; went fishing out of Matanzas; played cards and gambled in the government owned casinos and in illegally operated bars in Havana viejo. After a week, however, he'd run out of things to do; without steady companionship, he was lonely and made arrangements to fly back to Tampa.

The day before he left, Buck encountered Hardy Farkas, an old acquaintance whom he had known since both of them had lived in Chicago more than half a century before. Buck had started his construction business and Farkas, who was twenty years younger, was a runner for Barney Rothman, an alderman on the west side. Buck asked him what he was doing in Havana.

"The girls, what else?" said Hardy. "I've still got somethin' left. I'm not seventy yet! You?"

"I don't know what I've got left."

Farkas laughed. "I bet the ladies know. I'm livin' in Miami now, in the jewelry business. Last I heard you were retired somewhere in the Caribbean."

"Honduras."

"What do you do there?"

"Fish, mostly. I live on an island."

"Got an island girl? I could come visit sometime."

"Life's pretty slow there."

"If you're in Miami, look me up. I've got a store in Coral Gables."

Buck remembered when Barney Rothman was shot and killed in a motel in Cicero with somebody's wife. The word was that he was set up by one of his own people, probably Farkas. After that, Hardy went to work for Gus Madigan's gang. You couldn't trust anybody in Chicago in those days.

Buck flew back to Tampa and as he was on an escalator headed down to the baggage claim, he was bumped into by another passenger in a hurry. Buck fell, injuring his head, back, and legs. He was hospitalized and doctors told his daughter, Renalda, who also lived in Tampa, that he would most likely never walk again; also that her father's kidneys had failed, which would require treatment by dialysis. In addition, he may have incurred brain damage. His travelling days were over.

Renalda explained all of this to Buck as he drifted in and out of consciousness. On his third day in the hospital he told her that there was a Chinese shadow in his room, a veil covering his eyes. He was struggling, he said, to see through it.

"Your mother used to wear veils. Her eyes were a little crossed, she didn't like it when someone noticed. Where is she now?"

"In Madrid, she's remarried."

"I should go see her."

"Why Chinese?" Renalda asked. "Why a Chinese shadow?"

"On the Yangtze River, flowing from Kunlun Shan. I was sailing."

Buck tried to open his eyes but he could not.

"Let go, Colby," said Renalda.

When Renalda called Roy's mother, Kitty, who lived in Wisconsin, to tell her that Buck had died, Kitty said, "You know I'm fourteen years younger than my brother, I didn't see him very often, but I always enjoyed knowing that he was out somewhere in the world doing crazy things."

"You should go on thinking that way, Aunt Kitty, that he's still travelling."

"We all are, aren't we?"

After she hung up, Kitty repeated out loud, "Aren't we?"

" 'Aren't we' what?" asked her daughter, Sally, who had just walked into the room.

"Travelling."

"You going somewhere?"

"No, Sally, not yet."

Juana

Uncle Buck's Last Words

Roy's Uncle Buck was asleep in bed in a hospital. Roy sat on a chair next to the bed. Suddenly, Buck woke up and saw his nephew.

"Oh, Roy, I didn't know you were here."

"It's almost your birthday, Unk. You'll be ninety-three tomorrow."

"When was I born?"

"In 1911, in Chicago."

"I was dreaming that I was back in Africa, hiking alone through the bush. It must have been in Kenya, or maybe Tanzania. Yes, Tanzania, because Dar es Salaam was also in the dream. I had a small bag strapped over one shoulder, I'd packed a lunch. A native appeared and stood in front of me. He was very tall and half-naked. I greeted him in Swahili, 'Habari za asubuhi,' good morning, but he didn't reply. He stood still and stared down at me. I noticed that he had a knife stuck in his belt."

Habari za asubuhi

"What happened then?"

"I handed him my lunch."

"He didn't say anything?"

"No, he took it and disappeared back into the bush."

Buck closed his eyes.

"So will I," he said.

Parts Unknown

"Where are you, Unk?"

"I don't exactly know, Roy. When I was working building the railroad in the Yukon, a couple of the younger boys, neither of whom had ever been that far north before, said that after the job was over, and they were paid off, they would head toward parts unknown. That's as good an answer I can give you."

"Are you alone?"

The Commander with the Commandos